I0771802

"A songwriter and a singer, both chasing their country music dreams, discover love and unexpected success along the way."

Boots & Heartstrings

A Novella

Robert Starnes

Boots & Heartstrings

Published by Starnes Books LLC
Edited by Carpenter Editing Services, LLC

ISBN: 979-8-9892401-8-0 (sc)
ISBN: 979-8-9892401-9-7 (e)

Printed in the United States of America
First Printing, 2025

Table of Contents

Chapter 1

Open Mic Night

The Whiskey Factory is a bar where many of Eliott's clients have played in the past before becoming famous. It happens to be the place Eliott chose to sing tonight. The bar is packed for a Thursday night, but in Nashville, Tennessee, it was nothing unusual but for Eliott, his anxiety was rising to an all-new level. You see, twenty-six-year-old Eliott grew up in a small, conservative town in Tennessee. He is creative and sensitive and has always used songwriting as a form of expression, but singing on stage is a different story. Eliott has always been known as introverted, thoughtful, and a bit anxious, especially about performing and sharing his personal life. There is not much about Eliott that makes him stand out in a crowd. Eliott is medium height and has a slim build with messy dark hair and glasses. But his songwriting is one of the best in the industry.

Eliott is a shy but gifted songwriter who, while secretly penning lyrics for country music's biggest stars, dreams of performing them himself one day. He struggles with stage fright and the fear of revealing his true self to the world. Eliott has secrets of his own he fears will diminish his aspirations of being a huge country singer, so performing on stage is something he is not prepared to do.

Knowing his slot is about to come up, Eliott takes deep breaths and a shot of whisky to prepare himself for the stage. Tonight is the first night Eliott agreed to take the stage and sing one of his original songs, 'Dusty Roads,' for the crowded bar. Eliott was approached by one of the singers he writes for who has been encouraging Eliott to perform over the past year, and Eliott decided this night was his night. He sat at his table in a dark corner in the back of The Whiskey Factory, alone, secretly regretting agreeing to perform tonight. He knew he could not bail out now as it was almost his time to shine.

Eliott sat there with a slight buzz for a few minutes until the announcer came over the speakers announcing, "Please welcome to the stage Eliott, who will be performing his original song 'Dusty Roads', let's give him a big round of applause." Eliott stood up, shook off his nerves, and walked to the stage. His palms were sweating. With his anxiety rising, he thought he was going to pass out before reaching the stage, but he was able to keep it together. Eliott managed to walk to the center of the stage and take the microphone from the announcer. As soon as he grabbed the microphone, he looked out at the crowd and could not believe he was about to perform in front of so many people for the first time.

Eliott slowly moved the mic to his mouth and said his name and the name of the original song he was about to sing for them. His voice cracked a little during his opening and he could see the crowd notice, but he was not about to quit now. He worked so hard to get to where he is now, and he was going to sing his song.

Eliott began strumming his guitar and after a few bars, he opened his mouth and sang for the crowd. As he continued singing, he saw the crowd listening and moving in their seats. Seeing the crowd enjoying his song, he began to gain more confidence in his singing talent. His voice was perfectly on pitch and his words were so clear that the crowd was quickly learning the chorus and started singing along with him. Eliott began to have fun singing his song on stage for the first time. When he finished, the crowd began to stand and cheer for him. He knew he had only one slot for the night and knew an encore was out of the question, so he smiled and waved at the crowd while thinking of them as he walked off stage.

As Eliott is walking back to his table in the dark corner in the back of the Whiskey Factory, people begin to stand up as he walks by, clapping and shouting his name. Euphoria rushes over his body as he arrives at his table and takes a quick seat. This feeling puts a smile on his face, and everyone can see it. It is a sign of pure joy from his experience on stage. Before long, Eliott had drinks brought over to his table, paid for by many of the bar regulars. He began receiving so many free drinks that he told the waitress he could not accept any more drinks for the night, he had had enough.

Eliott's spectacular performance of 'Dusty Roads' was not only noticed by the regulars of the bar but also gained the attention of Sam. Sam is a twenty-eight-year-old from Austin, Texas, who moved to Nashville to pursue his dreams of being a big-time country music star. Eliott and Sam are total opposites. Sam is tall with a lean muscular build, a charismatic smile, and short blond hair. Unlike Eliott, Sam is outgoing, confident, and supportive, while Eliott is an introvert, shy, and anxious. Sam decides to go over to Eliott's table to introduce himself.

Sam can see how emotional Eliott is before he makes it to his table. Seeing Eliott excited about his performance makes Sam want to talk to him even more. Sam stops at Eliott's table and right away Eliott has something to say.

"Sorry, but I cannot accept any more free drinks tonight. I have enough now. I don't know how I will finish them all. But thank you for the offer," Eliott insistently tells Sam.

Sam is a little taken aback at the comment until he realizes Eliott's table is full of drinks waiting to be drunk. Eliott's comment to him as he walked up didn't stop Sam from doing what he set out to accomplish, to introduce himself to Eliott.

"I'm glad you are set for drinks, but I am not here to buy you a drink. I wonder if you have a moment to talk," Sam automatically responded.

"Oh, I am so sorry. I just thought… Never mind what I thought. How's your night going?" Eliott has a look of shame on his face replying to Sam.

"Don't worry about it. Let me introduce myself. My name is Sam Dawson, and I moved to Nashville about two years ago. I am a singer like you looking for my big break. I moved here from Austin hoping to become a big hit in country music, but I have not found that break just yet. I am not letting that stop me, so I go to every open mic I can find and sing. I know I have just thrown a lot at you about myself and if you don't remember, it's no problem. We can always come back to it later," Sam confidently tells Eliott.

Eliott takes a minute to recall anything Sam has just told him, but he unfortunately cannot remember anything except his name. Eliott seems stuck on Sam's height and build, causing him to ignore anything else he has said. Eliott is intimidated by Sam's appearance, but he quickly gathers his composure and snaps out of staring at Sam.

"Um, it's nice to meet you, Sam. I'm Eliott. Would you like to join me? As you can see, I have plenty of drinks that I cannot finish by myself," Eliott shyly asks Sam.

The pair smiled at each other before Sam agreed to join the table. As Sam settled in his seat, Eliott pushed a beer over for him, as a sign to say thank you for sitting. While they were drinking their beers, they were not conversing. They were enjoying the performance on stage. They listened until the current singer was finished before they spoke.

"So, what's your deal, Eliott? I have been going to every open mic night at every bar I can get a slot at, and I have never seen you around before," Sam inquisitively asks Eliott.

Eliott is taken back by Sam's bluntness and takes a moment to respond.

"I have been in Nashville for about seven years, but this is my first time singing at an open mic night. I am not one to be on center stage. I have issues with people looking at me, even if I am there for them to look at. I tend to stay out of the limelight," Eliott shyly replied to Sam.

"Really? You didn't seem nervous at all singing in the limelight tonight. If you have been in Nashville for seven years, how is this your first time singing?" Sam is curious to know more about Eliott.

Eliott smiled at Sam and said, "Well, I have been in Nashville for seven years writing songs for other artists. Many of them are country music superstars today, but don't ask me who because I can't tell you."

"Fair enough. That's awesome that you have been working in the industry for so many years and breaking out on your own," Sam expresses to Eliott.

"Well, it has taken me years to get to the point where I want to perform myself," Eliott replies to Sam.

"That's cool, not everyone is made for the spotlight, but they can always practice until they are ready like you did tonight. You sounded amazing and the lyrics to your song 'Dusty Roads' were so touching. I, like the rest of the bar, could feel your emotions through your singing. It was such a great performance. I hope you intend to keep singing at open mics, it would be a shame if you never got back up on stage," Sam honestly replied to Eliott.

"Thank you. Yes, I plan on singing more when I come up with some new music for me and not for my clients," Eliott happily replies to Sam.

"Since we are on the subject of your clients, how did you get into writing songs for other singers?" Sam inquisitively asks Eliott.

"Are you sure you want to hear the story? It's not as glamorous as you may think, it was more by accident, to be honest," Eliott modestly replies to Sam.

"Of course, I'm sure. I want to know all about you. You are an enigma to me. You moved to Nashville seven years ago and are only beginning to write and sing songs for yourself after years of writing songs for famous singers. Who wouldn't want to know more?" Sam honestly replies to Eliott.

"Well, it all started when I was in school. I used to write poems throughout grade school which all my teachers loved. My teachers loved my poems so much that they surprised me one year by telling me they had submitted some of my poetry for a national contest. That year I won. Not only had I won, but my poems were published in a poetry book, which became a bestseller. I had no idea my poems were as good as they thought, but apparently, the people doing the contest did and so did the people who bought the poetry book. So, when I got to high school I started writing songs in music class. I had written a new school song that was performed by the music class, and the students loved it. The school administration also loved it, so it became our new school song, and it still is," Eliott elaborates on his past writing experiences while taking a break to sip his beer.

Eliott could tell by the look on Sam's face he was drawn into his story and was enjoying it. Sam sipped his beer when Eliott did, not wanting to miss a word of his story. This made Eliott feel more comfortable with Sam.

"While I was writing songs in high school for our music class, we would play my songs at school competitions, and we started winning all of them. That was a first for our school. While we had competed in competitions for many, many years, our school had never won a single competition, until that year. That was in my freshman year. During my senior year, I had written several songs for us to sing at our competitions, and while we were still winning state competitions, we were also winning national competitions. Our competition winnings began to catch the attention of some small talent managers who had singers who needed songs to sing, so they reached out to the school. They wanted to know who wrote the songs we had been singing for the past four years. At first, our principal did not give out any information about the student and asked the talent managers if he could speak to the student first, before releasing any information. They were happy to wait for our principal to call them back. So many talent managers were calling the school. My principal finally came to me and told me what was going on and wanted my permission to let the talent managers know who I was. I went home one night and talked to my mother and father and discussed how my songwriting was getting noticed by talent managers who wanted to know who wrote the songs we performed at school. After a lengthy conversation with my parents, we let the principal release my parents' information if they wanted to contact the songwriter. I went to school the next day and told my principal what we decided, and he agreed with our decision," Eliott stops to take a breath and asks Sam if he wants a shot.

"Would you like a shot? People have already bought me several shots at the bar, and I don't want to offend anyone by not taking them."

"Sure, what are we having?"

"I'm not sure. I guess it will be a surprise."

Eliott leads Sam away from the table to the closest bar. Once at the bar, Eliott asks the bartender for two shots bought for him by his fans.

The bartender smiles at Eliott and turns around and pours two shots for him. Neither Sam nor Eliott watched as the bartender made their drinks because they were making small talk. After the bartender poured Eliott's shots, she set them down in front of them, interrupting their small talk. They both turn, look at the bartender, and grab a shot each. They clink glasses, cheer each other, and drink them down, quickly.

After they finish the shots, Eliott makes an awful face as if it did not like the shot he had just taken. Sam smiles at Eliott and chuckles under his breath.

"What's so funny?" Eliott asks Sam, feeling embarrassed.

"Nothing, I swear. Even though you were making an ugly face, it did not make you look ugly at all. You have such a unique look. You could never look ugly or funny, which makes it funny, to me that's all," Sam quickly explains the reason for his laughing.

Eliott gets embarrassed by what Sam has just told him, so he shyly turns away and begins walking back to the table, motioning for Sam to follow him, which Sam has no problem doing.

When they return to the table, Eliott grabs a beer off the table and takes a quick drink to get the taste of the shot out of his mouth. Then he continued telling his story.

"Now, where was I?" Eliott takes a minute to remember his place in his story. "Oh, I remember. Now that my principal was told how to handle the talent managers' calls, the calls at home began to pick up as well. We received several calls every week from different managers, all looking for someone to write songs for their clients. At first, my parents never told the managers I was a student at the school, only that I was the writer for the school's music department. My parents were not sure how the managers would respond if they knew I was only seventeen years old. The next thing I knew, I was getting requests for so many songs that my parents had to turn down several new managers. I was in high school, writing songs for semi-famous singers until the day one of the clients put one of my songs on their album. Once their album was released, it was released as number one on the charts with the song I wrote as the number one single of the album. By the time I graduated high school, I was under contract with six talent managers and writing songs for about a dozen of their clients. Every song I wrong shot the aspiring country music singer into superstardom. When I graduated college with my associate's degree in music, my contracts ended with the talent managers, and I was signed on with the actual artist. I never signed with a talent manager after that. I was exclusive with seven of the twelve artists I had written songs for for the last two years. Next thing you know, I was asked to move to Nashville by one of my clients, at their expense, so I could be closer and actually meet and write songs together. Since then, my clientele has increased, but I am no longer on any of my clients' contracts, they are under mine. This means I can stop writing songs for them at any time, which I have left a few, only so I could work on writing music for me to sing. Of course, I kept several other clients to keep my income coming in. So that's it. That is how I ended up in Nashville," Eliott ends his story with Sam, who was sitting in his chair hanging on every word Eliott spoke.

"Wow, what an amazing story. I can't believe it took you seven years to break away and make some time for yourself to perform your music, but I am beginning to understand. Thank you so much for telling me about how you got here." Sam leans back while smiling at Eliott.

With Eliott's story ended, the two continued talking while finishing all the drinks on Eliott's table. They talk for several hours about everything music-related; singers they like or dislike, songs they connect with, songs they don't connect with. Between talking, they enjoy listening to the other singers, their song choices, and performances. Having so many talented people in Nashville, almost every performer was on fire. There were great song choices and perfect pitches. Eliott was soaking in all their performances to see what he could do differently during his next open mic night.

Chapter 2

First Strings

As the evening dragged on, the bar announced its last call. Eliott and Sam look at each other as neither wants the night to end. Eliott is having such a great time. He wants to talk more with Sam. Before Eliott can ask Sam if they can continue talking for a bit longer, Sam interrupts Eliott's thoughts.

"Hey, I don't want to be too forward, but would you like to go for a cup of coffee or something?" Sam hopes Eliott agrees to go with him.

"I would love to get a cup of coffee with you. I have enjoyed talking with you. It's not often I am asked for my opinions about music." Eliott lies to Sam for the first time tonight, but he is not ready to tell him about what he does for a living.

"Great. I'm ready if you are," Sam tells Eliott with excitement.

Eliott stands up to follow Sam out of the bar. As the pair walks towards the door, Eliott gets praised by other guests who are also leaving. He thanks the bar owner and bartenders on his way out, which leaves Sam perplexed.

Sam wonders how Eliott knows everyone at the bar for someone who doesn't like the limelight. Sam thinks that for a shy guy, Eliott certainly knows a lot of people. Sam doesn't say anything to Eliott until they are on the sidewalk outside the bar.

"So, where do you want to get coffee?"

"Have you ever been to Dawn Café? It's the perfect venue for coffee this time of night," Eliott quickly responds to Sam.

"Never been. You lead the way," Sam tells Eliott as he waves his hand in a gesture for Eliott to take the lead.

Eliott takes the hint and starts walking towards Dawn Café. They walk a couple of blocks while still talking about anything music related. Eliott wonders if he and Sam will become friends, as he is enjoying his company. Eliott has not had many friends outside of work. This experience has been comforting for him tonight. They continue to chat along the way to the café.

Eliott walks up to the door of the café and holds it open for Sam. Sam enters the café and notices how many other singers are there. Almost everyone they have heard sing tonight is there. As they walked into the café, even though guests noticed Eliott, they didn't praise him as when he finished singing earlier or when they were leaving the bar. That put them both more at ease, giving them space to find a seat. Eliott found a table in the back of the café, which was his typical fashion, to avoid as many people as possible.

Sam and Eliott are having a light conversation while they wait for their waitress. The waitress comes to their table, and they both order coffee. After she leaves, they continue their previous conversation until she returns.

"Thank you, Rayna," Eliott tells the waitress as she fills their coffee cups and walks away.

"You must come here pretty often," Sam instinctively questions Eliott.

"Why do you think I come here often?" Eliott quickly replies.

"You seem to know everyone in Nashville. You know the bartenders and the owner at the bar. You even know the name of the waitress here. How often do you go out?" Sam inquisitively asks.

"I can tell you I go out a little bit, but it's not what you think. I may have written a few songs for some other singers in the past, and people only know me because of those singers. Nothing more," Eliott clarifies to Sam.

"Would I know any of the singers?" Sam playfully asks Eliott.

"I don't like talking about songs I have written for other singers. Can we change the subject, please?" Eliott is embarrassed about his previous work.

"Sorry. I didn't mean to upset you," Sam apologizes to Eliott.

"No need to apologize, it's no big deal," Eliott declares to Sam.

A moment of silence takes over their table before Sam speaks again.

"Eliott, can I ask you a question?"

"Sure, what's on your mind?" Eliott responds.

"I am wondering if you would like to work on a collaboration with me. I realize we just met, but I loved your music tonight and feel we could work well on a song. I don't know if you have heard me sing or any of my songs, but my style is close to yours. We have something to say and a way to say it with music. If you took a chance on listening to my songs, you might find we have a lot in common," Sam blurts out to Eliott.

Eliott is surprised by Sam's proposal but is intrigued at the same time. He takes a minute to think about it.

"Can I think about it? I have a lot going on right now, and I am unsure if I have the time to add a new project. Let's enjoy our coffee and conversation for now," Eliott shyly responds to Sam.

"Of course, you can think about it. I didn't mean to put you on the spot. Regardless, I would love to see you again. I have had such a great time tonight. I don't want it to end," Sam insists to Eliott.

Eliott is grateful that Sam is so understanding and not pressing the issue. He relaxes as the morning moves on, drinking coffee and having fun conversations with Sam. Eliott lets time pass. Before Eliott notices the time, it is past 3 A.M., which is super late for him.

"Sam, I hate to interrupt this night or morning, I should say, but I really must be going home. I have an early morning today," Eliott expresses to Sam.

"Oh, wow! I didn't even notice the time. I am sorry I kept you out so late. I hope we can meet again tomorrow. I would like to hear your thoughts about a potential collaboration," Sam brings up his previous request to Eliott.

"Of course. Should we exchange numbers? I can text you tomorrow," Eliott asks for Sam's number.

"Yes, I would love it if we could meet tomorrow," Sam eagerly answers Eliott as they swap phone numbers. Once they had each other's phone numbers, Eliott was the first to say goodnight to Sam before leaving him at their table, forgetting to pay the tab.

Eliott and Sam make it safely to their respective homes and go to bed. Both have plans for a busy day.

Eliott wakes up around 8 A.M. and heads straight for his bathroom. He knows he has an early morning session with another well-known singer in about an hour. He rushes to make himself presentable for his client before he hears a knock on his door.

Eliott answers his door, knowing who is waiting on the other side, reminding him of how particular this artist is. He doesn't know when to expect their session to end for the day so he can see Sam, but he knows it will be late.

While Eliott is working with his client, Sam is paying his dues in the country music industry. He is an intern at a local country music label in Nashville. Even though Sam is outgoing, he has never dared to submit his music to his employer. Sam has reservations about his personal life, which he lets others know through his lyrics. He feels his label will not take him as a serious country singer.

The relentless day keeps them from having time to text one another, leading Eliott to think Sam has reconsidered. Eliott decides to take matters into his own hands for once.

Eliott takes out his phone and pulls up Sam's number to text him. As he looks at his phone, he suddenly receives a text notification from Sam.

Sam: *Hey Eliott, it's me, Sam, from last night. I'm sorry I haven't texted you today, but I am having a crappy day. What time do you get off work?*

Eliott: *No worries. I am having a crappy day as well. I'm off at 9 P.M. tonight. Will it be too late for us to meet?*

Sam: *No. 9 P.M. is perfect. I will be off soon, giving me enough time to stop at home and get ready.*

Eliott: *Ready? For what?*

Sam: *To meet up with you.*

Eliott: *Oh. Where are we meeting?*

Sam: *How about the same place as last night? Dawn Café?*

Eliott: *Sounds good. I'll see you there!*

The text messages between them ended on a positive note for Eliott. He now needs to finish with his client.

Sam works for another hour before he is off work. Upon leaving work, Sam rushes home to prepare for his meetup with Eliott. He wants to make a good impression on Eliott because he genuinely wants him to agree to a collaboration. Even though they talked last night, he wants to be more formal for this meeting. He believes collaborating with Eliott will boost his career to a higher level since they have such a close style of writing songs.

While Sam is home getting ready, Eliott is still working with his client, trying to wrap up their session. Eliott's client is not one to feel rushed, so Eliott must be cautious with how to end the session on a positive note. Eliott decides to tell his client he was just notified that a friend was taken to the hospital, and he must leave to meet them there, so they should begin wrapping up for the day. Eliott tells his client how well the day has gone and conveys how he can't wait until their next session. His client soaks up all the accolades from Eliott, so he is not upset about ending the day. They wrap up, his client leaves, and Eliott has enough time to prepare for his meeting with Sam.

Eliott finishes the final touches on his attire for the evening: a pair of blue jeans, a red button-up western-style shirt, glasses, and his cowboy hat to cover his dark, messy hair. Like Sam, Eliott also wants to make a good impression. They both know meeting someone at a bar late at night does not always make the meetup the next time any easier.

Sam is the first to make it to Dawn Café and grabs a seat for them at a booth in the back. He remembers Eliott likes to sit away from other people, mainly in the back of the bar and even at Dawn Café, like early this morning before they both went home. Sam orders water for himself as he waits for Eliott to arrive.

Eliott arrives at Dawn Café a few minutes after 9. As he enters, he notices Sam at a booth. Eliott casually walks over to Sam, but before he can sit, Sam stands up to greet Eliott. As he stands up, Eliott can't help but notice a rainbow pin on his cowboy hat. Eliott is surprised by the pin and is uncertain how to act around Sam, but he puts it out of his mind for now.

"I'm so glad you agreed to meet with me tonight. I have been waiting all day to see you," Sam greets Eliott.

"No problem. I am glad to see you too," Eliott shyly responds.

The two of them shake hands and take their seats in the booth. Before they have time to begin talking more with each other, they are interrupted by a waitress.

"Good evening, boys. What can I get y'all to drink?"

"I'll have a Dr. Pepper, please," Eliott orders first.

"I'll have the same," Sam tells the waitress.

"Two Dr. Peppers coming up. I'll be back in a few with your drinks to give you some time to look at the menu," the enthusiastic waitress informs them before she turns around and heads to the counter.

"Have you had time to eat today? Should we get something?" Sam asks Eliott.

"I'm not hungry, but if you are, order something."

Sam takes a moment to look at the menu but ultimately decides not to order anything. He is ready to see if he can convince Eliott to work with him on a song or more.

"I'm good. How about we get straight to business?" Sam asks Eliott.

"Sounds good to me. Could you share more about your background and how you began singing and writing your own songs?" Eliott asks Sam as an icebreaker.

"Well, I was born and raised in Austin, Texas. I moved here to Nashville five years ago. I thought it would be easier for me to make it big in the country music industry if I lived closer to where it all happens, but it has not been so easy," Sam begins to tell Eliott a little about his background.

"What seems to be your biggest challenge in country music since moving to Nashville?" Eliott wants to hear more about Sam's music background to help him decide if he will collaborate with him.

"Well, I can tell you that being an out and proud gay male country singer closes more doors than it opens. I have been to a few local labels that have heard my songs and invited me for a meet and greet. Just as I thought things were going well, as soon as they heard I was gay and proud, the meeting would end. I am thanked for my time and told they will be in touch. They are never in touch again," Sam expands on his challenges in Nashville.

"I am sorry to hear you have been going through those things. Let me ask you, do you want to collaborate with me because you think working with me will open more doors for you or even some that were closed on you?" Eliott asks Sam with a serious expression.

Sam reads Eliott's face and quickly feels ashamed that he was thinking such things.

"No way, Eliott. I do not know much about you except from hearing you sing last night and our talk early this morning. I wanted to see if we could write together because I loved the song you sang and how well you sang it. I am only asking based on your pure talent for singing and songwriting, nothing more. I am sorry if I come across as someone who wants to use you to get ahead. That was never my intention," Sam clarifies his actions towards Eliott.

Eliott leans back in his seat and looks at Sam with a stern, hard look before replying to him.

"I'm sorry, Sam. I don't mean to insult you or question your motives for wanting to work with me. I can be a little harsh at times. Working in this industry can do that to you. Please forgive my arrogance," Eliott begins apologizing.

Sam is relieved to hear Eliott apologize. He thought he had ruined everything between them so early in their friendship.

"There is no need to apologize. I understand what you mean by the industry changing you. I must admit that I have changed some too since moving here," Sam accepts Eliott's apology.

"You changed? How so? If you don't mind me asking," Eliott openly asks.

"To be honest with you, I have had to change many things about myself. While I have always been an out and proud gay man and an advocate within the LGBTQ+ community, I have dialed down my outness and have shied away from the community that accepts me for who I am and not what they want me to be," Sam answers Eliott honestly.

Eliott is saddened to hear the struggles Sam has been going through trying to make it big. Deep down, he understands why and is moved by Sam's story. He decides, at that moment, to collaborate with him.

"I am sorry to hear you have been having a hard time here in Nashville, but there are other LGBTQ+ country music singers here. More than you know," Eliott reassures Sam. "They may not be as popular as straight singers, but they are popular in their community."

"I know, but I am worried about becoming one of those artists. I want to be known by everyone, not just the community," Sam replies.

"I know what you mean, and I want to try and help with that. I will agree to work with you to see what we can come up with, but I can't guarantee what we do will make you an instant star. I hope you can agree to those terms," Eliott tells Sam enthusiastically.

"Are you serious about collaborating with me? I have a feeling we can do great things together. I promise I won't let you down," Sam exclaims.

Chapter 3

Late Night Lyrics

Sam and Eliott plan to meet every night for the rest of the week. They plan on meeting tomorrow at Sam's place so he can share some of his music with Eliott. Sam hasn't performed in front of Eliott yet and wants to share some of his songs with him. Sam hopes that when Eliott hears his songs, he will not regret his decision to work with him, and the thought excites him. They finish today's meeting with a plan for the rest of the week, and then Sam and Eliott part ways.

Now that the plans for the week are complete, Sam decides to go out a little to celebrate. Since Eliott has left already Sam heads to another bar in town holding an open mic night, one he has sung at before but is not on the list for tonight. He figures he may go and listen to others trying to make it big and show support for them.

Sam walks into the bar and notices it is not as busy as it usually is on a Friday night. He walks to the bar and orders a drink before taking refuge at an empty table nearby. Sam sits alone at his table, watching and admiring the performers going up. He has always been passionate about music, regardless of the genre. As he enjoys his drink and entertainment, Jimmy, the event coordinator, approaches him.

"Hey, Sam, would you like to fill a spot for me tonight? I just had someone vomit and leave, and I have to fill their spot. You would be helping me out," Jimmy pleads with Sam.

"Anything for you, Jimmy. You have helped me out in the past. When do I go on?" Sam inquires.

"Well, you are next, but I don't see your guitar with you. Can you still perform without one? If you need one, let me know so I can try to round one up for you," Jimmy quickly tells Sam with desperation in his eyes.

"If you can find me one, that would be great," Sam accepts Jimmy's offer.

Jimmy quickly runs in search of a guitar for Sam. Sam goes to the bar and orders another beer and shot. He wants to get a buzz to shake off his nerves. Even though Sam has performed in so many places, he still gets nervous. He takes his shot at the bar, then grabs his beer to bring back to his table.

While Sam quickly downs his beer, Jimmy comes rushing up to him with a guitar in hand.

"Will this work for you? This is all I could find on such short notice."

"As long as it has strings, I will make it work. How much time do I have?"

"None, so chug your beer and make your way up to the stage so I can introduce you," Jimmy instructs Sam.

Sam does as Jimmy instructs, chugs his beer, slams the empty bottle on the table, and makes his way up to the stage. As he approaches, Jimmy announces him.

"Thank you, Brian, for an amazing performance tonight. Everyone, please give Brian a big round of applause. Next on stage, we have Sam Dawson playing one of his favorites for you. Let's give him a warm welcome."

The crowd goes crazy with Sam being introduced as the next singer. He has performed at this bar so many times everyone knows him. Hearing his regulars cheering him on sets his mood for the song he is about to perform. Sam is performing a new song he wrote and is ready for feedback from the crowd.

Sam takes the stage and as soon as he strums the guitar strings the crowd goes silent, as if they were put in a trance by Sam's finger action on the guitar strings. They remain quiet until Sam's mouth opens, and he begins to sing. As soon as Sam lets out the first note in his song the crowd starts screaming, loving every minute. Sam continues his song with perfect pitch and never misses a beat. With the bar crowd dancing on the floor and whooping and hollering, Sam is getting the feedback he was hoping for on his new song.

Sam finishes his set and takes a bow for his fans. He is overjoyed with the outcries from the bar. He felt his new song would be something good, he never expected the bar to enjoy it as much as he did. Sam also felt the bar would not have liked it as much if they knew the real meaning of his song. Sam exits the stage and takes in all the affirmations he receives from the bar as he heads back to his table.

Sitting back at his table and coming down from his high from performing, he is approached by someone he knows. Eliott walks up to his table and interrupts his appreciation of the moment.

Sam looks at Eliott and asks, "What are you doing here? I thought you were going home."

"I could ask you the same thing. I have to say, I am glad I didn't go home tonight. If I had, I wouldn't have been able to hear you sing just now. You have an amazing voice and your song was beautiful," Eliott states.

Sam smiles at Eliott and asks him to take a seat. Eliott accepts the offer but expresses he can only stay for a little while. He explained he has an early session tomorrow with the same client from today. Eliott mentions how he left early for their meeting, and how he had to blow off his client for the rest of their session.

Sam agrees to Eliott's terms and hands him one of the beers that were left on his table as he was singing. Eliott takes the beer, and they sit back and enjoy the short time they have together.

It wasn't long before Eliott excused himself from Sam's table to head home. They say their farewells to each other. Eliott leaves and Sam chooses to go as well. He knows tomorrow will be the same kind of day as they all have been, but he also knows he now has something to look forward to, his first session with Eliott at his place. He wants to get home tonight so he can clean up his place before going to bed.

Sam makes it home, cleans the flat he is renting, and still makes it to bed at a decent hour, around 2 AM.

Eliott rises before sunup, knowing he must be on time and prepared for his client. He does not want to have any issues today with said client, which he usually does. Eliott does not want anything to cause him to be late with Sam tonight.

Sam is going through some of the same issues as Eliott today, except he doesn't wake up until later. Sam knows his day will be the same as every other day at work, doing coffee runs, answering phones, scheduling appointments, and getting lunch orders. Sam's day is predictable, so he knows he will be at his place before Eliott arrives.

Sam ends his day just like every other day, clocking out and heading home. As he arrives at his flat, he hurriedly rushes inside to shower and change his clothes. Sam takes a steamy hot shower, letting the steam open the pores on his dark smooth body. Enjoying his shower, Sam loses track of time. Before he realizes how late it has become, he hears a knock on his door. Startled by the insistent knocking, Sam grabs a towel, wrapping it around his hot wet body, and rushes to open the door.

Eliott is standing outside Sam's door when he opens it. At the sight of Sam in his towel, Eliott suddenly feels flush. Unsure as to why he is having such a feeling seeing Sam this way, Eliott quickly shakes his head, diverting his eyes away from Sam, and asks, "What are you wearing, Sam?" Eliott asks in a shocking tone.

Sam is surprised to see Eliott arriving so early, but he is also thrilled.

"Sorry, Eliott, I wasn't expecting you this early. I was in the middle of a shower when you knocked. I rushed out of the bathroom so you wouldn't leave. Won't you come in?" Sam, being body-positive, has no problem answering his door in a towel.

"Early? I am right on time. How long were you in the shower?" Eliott inquisitively asks.

"Really? Wow, I must have dozed off briefly as the hot water warmed the room. So, are you coming in?" Sam coyly responds.

"It depends. Are you planning on getting dressed?" Eliott replies in embarrassment.

Sam smiles and gives Eliott a soft laugh before he responds. "Of course, I am going to get dressed unless you have something else in mind," Sam smirks at Eliott. "I'm kidding. I'm going to change. I'm getting cold standing in my towel with the door open."

Eliott acknowledges Sam's request to come in so he can shut the door to get dressed. Once they are in Sam's flat, Sam indicates to Eliott to have a seat on the couch as he goes to get dressed. Eliott takes a seat and Sam exits the room.

Sam heads to his room to dry off and get dressed, but he doesn't shut his bedroom door, out of habit of living alone for so long. He already has the clothes he intends to wear sitting on his bed, all he needs to do is dry off and dress. Sam takes his towel from around his waist to dry off his wet body. He dries his hair first before rubbing his towel over his arms, chest, and back, and then bends over so he can dry off his legs. While Sam is getting ready, Eliott patiently waits for him to return.

Eliott looks around Sam's flat, trying to learn more about his lifestyle. As he looks around the room, Eliott's eyes move towards Sam's bedroom with the open door. Eliott glances into Sam's room just as Sam is bending over drying his legs with the towel. Eliott is surprised how Sam is so confident to stand naked with his bedroom door open while someone is sitting right outside of the room. Eliott is not aware of how long he is looking at Sam's nude body, but it is long enough for Sam to turn around to get dressed. Sam is now facing Eliott, who has a full view of Sam's body. Eliott is impressed by Sam's physique, especially in comparison to his slim build. However, he does not notice that Sam is looking directly at him. When their eyes meet, Eliott quickly turns away and focuses on his phone.

"Sam, can I ask you a question?" Eliott wonders out loud.

"Sure, what's up?" Sam responds to Eliott while pulling up his underwear, snapping the waistband against his bare body.

"How are you so comfortable dressing in front of someone you don't know? I could never be so brazen," Eliott honestly inquires.

"Why not? We are both adults and have the same body parts, so who cares who sees me naked? It doesn't bother me one bit, but if it bothers you, I can close my door."

"No need to close your door on my account. It is your flat, and you have every right to dress the way you want and in front of whomever you want. I just wish I was more confident like you are. It was just a question, no big deal," Eliott suddenly wants to end the topic he had brought up.

Sam is not offended by Eliott's question and quickly throws on a tight tee shirt and loose gray sweatpants before returning to the living room.

"Okay, so are you ready to start working on something?" Sam is ready to start writing songs.

Eliott walks over to Sam, who is sitting at a table on the side of the room. As he settles in a seat, Sam begins showing Eliott some of the things he has written in the past that he never finished. They quickly start brainstorming more lyrics to match what Sam has already penned to paper. That continues until around midnight. Eliott tells Sam he needs to leave because he has work in the morning. They part ways until their next writing session.

Sam and Eliott continue meeting at Sam's flat for the next several months, creating new lyrics and music for their work. On the nights the pair can't meet, Sam hits the open mic nights at his usual haunts.

During their time together, the two share life experiences and values, particularly about authenticity in their music and lives. Their nights are filled with creativity, gradually turning professional respect into personal affection.

The more they hang out, the more Sam's feelings for Eliott grow. Since Eliott is not out or given any verbal acknowledgment of being gay, Sam doesn't press the issue. He knows if Eliott is in the closet, he will have to come out on his own, not be forced to come out. So, Sam decides to wait.

Even though Sam has growing feelings for Eliott, he values their friendship and working together more than having a relationship with him. The art they are creating with music is something they both love, so they decide to try out one of their songs at an open mic night. Sam is so excited he reaches out to Jimmy, the open mic coordinator at a bar where he sings and asks if he could fill a spot for his next open mic night. They don't have to wait long because Jimmy has an open spot the next night and gives it to Sam and Eliott.

With the excitement of performing one of their new songs tomorrow, they decide to celebrate. They drop what they are doing. Sam grabs Eliott's hand and pulls him up from the table to lead him out the front door. Eliott did not seem to mind when Sam grabbed his hand, as they were close friends; it was nothing out of the ordinary for them. They ran to the nearest bar to grab some drinks.

The two keep drinking shots and beers until they are more than buzzed. They have such a good time that neither wants the night to end, so they leave the bar and head to the corner store. They grab a twelve-pack of beer and head to Sam's flat. They are both off work tomorrow, so drinking tonight is the perfect night to tie one on.

Drinking at Sam's goes on until 4 AM, and Eliott is too drunk, at this point, to walk home, which Sam notices. Sam offers Eliott his couch to sleep on for tonight, and Eliott accepts with much gratitude. Sam gets a blanket and pillow for his guest. Eliott runs to the bathroom while Sam gathers the things for Eliott.

"Hey, Eliott, do you need something to sleep in?" Sam yells out to Eliott in the bathroom.

Unsure of what to say to Sam, Eliott freezes because he hasn't thought about pajamas.

"No, I'm good. I'll sleep in my clothes or take a page out of your playbook and sleep naked!" Eliott jokingly shouts out of the bathroom, laughing the entire time.

Sam laughs at Eliott's joke and makes the couch up for Eliott for the night before heading off to his room to get ready for bed.

Eliott comes out of the bathroom, still laughing at his own joke, almost falling as he stumbles to the couch. Eliott falls on the couch, fully dressed.

Sam, ready for bed, sees Eliott lying on top of the blanket, fully dressed. Sam heads to the living room to help make Eliott more comfortable.

Eliott sees Sam out of the corner of his eye heading his way, and Sam is naked, walking towards him. This time, Eliott does not shake his head or look away. He kept his eyes focused on Sam's perfectly shaped, tall, muscular, hard body, getting closer to him. Eliott is uncertain what Sam is about to do, but he believes he is ready for anything.

Sam makes it to Eliott and reaches down next to his body, reaching for the blanket to pull over him, but Eliott stops him suddenly. Eliott changes his mind about sleeping in his clothes for the night and begins to try to take his shirt off. Struggling to unbutton his shirt, he asks Sam for help.

"Sam, can you help me take my shirt off, please? I can't sleep in this hot shirt."

Sam thinks nothing about it, helps Eliott with his buttons, and removes his shirt for him.

"You need any more help, Eliott? Or can you handle the rest of your clothes?" Sam asks, making sure Eliott will be comfortable for the night.

"Can you take my boots and socks off while I unbutton my pants? I can't reach my feet right now," Eliott giggles as he says the last part.

Sam, without questioning Eliott, moves to a position at the end of the couch and pulls off his boots and socks. All the while, Eliott has already begun trying to remove his pants but failing miserably. Sam can't keep watching Eliott push and pull his pants, trying to wiggle them off his body, so Sam reaches for the ends of Eliott's pants legs and pulls them off in one quick motion. Unknowingly to Sam, Eliott isn't wearing any underwear and now they are both naked, staring at each other.

Sam softly moves his hands down to Eliott's waist, grabs the blanket beneath his body, and pulls it past Eliott's feet. Then he slowly pulls the blanket back up, covering up Eliott's fully exposed body.

At first, Eliott is surprised by Sam's actions but quickly falls asleep.

Once Eliott is covered up, Sam turns down the lights and walks back to his bedroom, leaving the door open as usual. Little did Sam know Eliott was not asleep but was watching him walk back to his room. Sam falls on his bed on top of his covers without thinking anything of it. It's how he sleeps at night.

Both of them were drunk and passed out for the night. Nothing happened during the night except for the constant snoring from both of them.

As the morning sun shines through the flat windows, Sam wakes up before Eliott. After using the bathroom, Sam goes to the kitchen to cook breakfast. After a long night of drinking, the first thing Sam usually needs is food. Thinking Eliott will feel the same way when he gets up, he cooks enough for them both. After breakfast is ready and the table set, Sam walks to Eliott to wake him up.

Eliott must have had a rough night's sleep since his blanket was pushed to the end of the couch. Eliott's bare butt facing Sam. Sam smiles at Eliott's cute little butt and nudges Eliott by his arm to wake him. Eliott begins to move around and turn over on the couch, now giving Sam the full monte with a morning salute, then quickly realizes he is naked.

"Oh my god. I am so sorry I am lying naked on your couch. What happened to my clothes?" Eliott asks Sam, obviously embarrassed.

Sam told Eliott how he ended up naked and how nothing happened, how he covered him and went to bed himself. Sam finishes explaining the night to Eliott, walks into his bedroom, slips into a pair of loose-fitting shorts, and brings Eliott a pair.

"I figure you want something to wear while we eat breakfast," Sam throws the extra pair of shorts over to Eliott before heading to the dining room table.

Eliott thanks Sam for the shorts, and as soon as the coast is clear, he quickly slips them on. Dressed now, Eliott joins Sam at the table. Breakfast is quiet at first, but before they know it, they are talking about music once more and discussing what they want to do today.

Chapter 4

Harmony

After breakfast, they decide to stay in and continue to write music. They bounce ideas off each other about what they want to say in this song and agree on a duet. It's not often to have a duet between two men in Nashville, or country music as a whole, but they want to try. They write and write all day long, coming up with lyrics and melodies until they feel they have something worth singing. They practice their duet at Sam's place, singing and playing their guitars, adjusting as they play. Once they feel they have something worth sharing, they decide to try it out tonight.

Since it's a Tuesday and they have been writing all day, they know any place they go tonight will have a slot open. They chose a bar they usually do not go to, so if the song sucks, no one they know would be there. That gives them an excuse to perform it the same day as writing it. With the duet finished, they pack up their guitars and head to the spot where they are performing tonight.

The place they are going to sing at tonight is a little way away from Sam's, so they call a car service to drive them there, as neither of them has a car. Standing outside Sam's building, Eliott feels compelled to say something about last night to Sam.

"Sam, can I ask you a question?"

"Sure, Eliott, what's on your mind?"

"Nothing really, I just wanted to say how sorry I am for how you found me on your couch this morning. I never sleep nude at home, and I shouldn't have slept that way on your couch."

Sam has been thinking about seeing Eliott lying on his couch in his birthday suit all morning but was too afraid to mention it. Sam didn't want to say anything that could get in between their friendship.

"Eliott, you have nothing to be sorry about. I didn't mind you sleeping comfortably on my hard couch. I know it's not the most comfortable and can be difficult to sleep on, so if you need to be naked to sleep on it, so be it."

"It was not that hard," Eliott replies.

"It looked hard to me."

"Sam! That is not what I was talking about. That is a normal reaction for someone my age and yours to wake up like that!"

"Eliott, I am joking with you. I know what you were talking about. I am trying to make light of the situation. Honestly, it did not bother me at all. You may have noticed I am a body-positive person, so being nude does not bother me, and it shouldn't bother you. You are hot, if you don't mind me saying so," Sam clears the air with Eliott.

Eliott blushes at Sam's comment about him being hot because no one ever tells him such things. Eliott has always been uncomfortable with his body and shy about being nude in front of anyone.

"You think I'm hot?" Eliott asks Sam.

"Of course I do! Don't you feel hot?" Sam replies.

"Never!"

"Well, you should. You have nothing to be ashamed of about your body. With me around, you will learn how to accept yourself for who you are, like me! If you can learn how to love yourself more, you will find doors open up for you in other ways," Sam explains to Eliott.

"What do you mean, other doors?"

"Easy. You learn to love yourself and others will love you as well. I assume you are single since we have been hanging out writing for over two months, and you have never mentioned a girlfriend or boyfriend," Sam states facts he knows about Eliott.

Eliott begins to reply to Sam, but their car pulls up to take them to the bar where they are performing tonight.

"Hold that thought, Eliott, our car is here."

Eliott looks up from his hand and sees the car approaching. As the car stops, Sam reaches for the door handle of the back seat and opens it, allowing Eliott to get in first. Once Eliott is in, Sam jumps in the back seat and shuts the door. Sam jumped into the back seat so fast he nearly sat on Eliott's lap. Eliott was not quick to scoot over.

Sam is now sitting so close to Eliott that their legs are touching, and Sam's hand lands on Eliott's lap by accident.

"Sorry about that," Sam tells Eliott as he moves his hand from Eliott's lap. "You didn't leave me much room to sit."

"Don't worry about it. It was an accident."

"It really was, I promise. Now, what were you about to say before the car pulled up?"

"I can't remember. What were we talking about?" Eliott forgot their earlier conversation after Sam's hand placement incident.

"Talking about you having someone in your life, besides me, of course," Sam reminds Eliott of their conversation before their car arrived.

"Oh, yes. You are correct, I am single. I have been single for some time now. To be honest, I have never had a serious long-term relationship."

"You have never had a relationship is what I am gathering. Not even in school?" Sam seems surprised about Eliott's confession.

"Nope, I was more focused on school than relationships in high school and college. School was more important to me then, or that's at least how my parents explained it to me," Eliott tells Sam.

Sam looks at Eliott with sadness in his eyes. He can't believe Eliott's parents told him his education was more important than being loved. Before Sam can address the issues with what Eliott has just told him, their car stops in front of the bar.

Before Sam reaches for the car door to open it and let them out, he grabs Eliott's hand and gives it a slight squeeze letting him know he supports him, regardless of what his parents had told him.

Eliott does not understand why Sam has grabbed his hand, but he feels it is an innocuous moment, and as soon as Sam exits the car, he follows. Now that they are out of the car, Sam leads the way to the entrance, where they are met by a super straight bouncer who almost doesn't let them in because he knows Sam.

"What's going on, Sam? Why is this guy giving us a hard time getting in?"

"It's a long story but don't worry because I know the owner and he will be reprimanded by the owner tomorrow," Sam reassures Eliott.

Eliott is curious as to why the door guy acted like he did when they first got to the door. He decides to wait until they are at a table before asking

Sam more about it. As they walk into the club, Sam lets go of Eliott's hand and makes his way straight to the bar. Eliott continues walking in Sam's direction until he reaches the bar beside him. As Eliott walks up, Sam has already ordered a beer and shot for them both.

"Here, Eliott, take this!"

"What is it?"

"Just drink it. You will love it!"

Without any more questions, Eliott grabs the shot, raises it to clink Sam's shot, turns it up to his mouth, and drinks it. As he finishes the shot, he makes a disgusting face.

"Why are you making that face?" Sam jokingly asks Eliott.

"This is the worst thing I ever drank. What is it?" Eliott questions Sam while making a gagging sound and dry heaving.

"It's Jameson, an Irish whisky," Sam quickly replies.

"Why is it so hot? I like my shot's at least chilled!" Eliott confesses to Sam.

"Sorry, I've heard it's the best way to take it. Next time I'll let you pick the shot," Sam replies to Eliott laughing.

Eliott just shook his head and began walking away from the bar. He continues walking until he reaches an empty table. Eliott takes a seat, claiming the empty table, and sits there until Sam comes and sits across from him.

"I'm sorry about the shot, Eliott. I hope you are not mad. We are here to perform our song for the first time, so I wanted to be sure you had a good buzz before going on stage. Trust me, warm Jameson is a great way to get a quick buzz. Speaking of a buzz, how are you feeling?"

"Now that you mention it, I am doing very well. How long do we have before we go on?"

Before Sam can reply, Jimmy walks over to their table.

"Jimmy! Thank you again for letting us fill a spot tonight. We appreciate it," Sam shouts out to Jimmy, the open mic coordinator for tonight.

"You have about an hour before going on, is that okay? You will go on at eleven," Jimmy replies to Sam while looking at Eliott.

"Sorry, this is Eliott. We will be performing a song together tonight," Sam introduces Jimmy to Eliott.

Jimmy and Eliott exchange greetings before Jimmy excuses himself to head back to the stage to announce the next singer.

Now, with Jimmy gone, Eliott decides to ask Sam about the incident that happened at the door when they first got there.

"Sam, can I ask you a question?"

"Sure, what's on your mind?"

"What's the story about you and the door guy?"

Sam looks at Eliott and gives him a little smile before asking him.

"Well, one night, Eric, the door guy, was giving me shit about being gay, cracking jokes with anyone who would listen to him. It got so bad one night that when he went to the bathroom, I followed him. Once we were alone in the bathroom, Eric made a pass at me. He grabbed my hand and put it on his hard cock. I quickly pulled away, but he restrained me and kept holding my hand on it. Then he told me I was going home with him that night. I agreed with him just to make him let me go, but he got really upset when I left alone as soon as I left the bathroom. From then on, he started trying to spread rumors about me being a male escort, but no one believed him because they all knew me. Since then, he has given me a hard time whenever I come here, afraid I would tell others the truth. But I never have, until now," Sam revealed to Eliott.

Eliott takes Sam's explanation to heart, hearing how hurtful another person was to him. Eliott regards Sam as such a loving and friendly person it is hard for him to fathom hearing someone doing that to him.

pg. 58

"Sam, I am so sorry I asked. I can't believe he did that to you. What an ass!"

"Don't worry about it, it was months ago. Now, let's get back to tonight! This is our night, not his," Sam pleads with Eliott to drop the subject.

Eliott takes the hint from Sam to drop the subject and turns their conversation around to tonight.

"You know I can't go on unless I have at least one more shot," Eliott tells Sam.

"Like I told you earlier, you get to pick the shot this time. So what are we having?" Sam reminds Eliott.

Eliott does not say anything to Sam and gets up and walks away from the table towards the bar. He orders a couple of shots and as soon as they are poured, he grabs them and takes them back to their table.

"Here, drink this," Eliott smiles at Sam as he hands him one of the shots. "Don't ask what it is, just drink it."

Sam shows Eliott he is not afraid of taking an unknown shot, pulls the shot glass up to his mouth, and shoots the drink down. Eliott does the same.

Once they both finish their shot, Sam looks over to Eliott and smiles.

"Jager Bombs? My favorite. Thanks, Eliott!" Sam yells out.

The two continue to drink their beers and laugh at each other until Jimmy comes back over to let them know they are on next.

With Jimmy's words, Sam and Eliott look at each other quickly, have a good laugh, and make their way up to the stage.

"Are you ready to sing our song?" Sam asks as he sees how nervous Eliott is.

"I am ready. Let's do this," Eliott replies with a huge smile.

Jimmy begins to announce them to the stage, and before he can finish, Eliott runs up onto the stage with Sam behind him. They both have their guitars in hand and mics right in front of them. As soon as Jimmy finishes, the pair quickly begin picking at their guitars.

They begin playing the intro, which is slow in the beginning but speeds up later. They continue playing and singing to the point where the crowd is loving every moment of it. Their harmony is pitch-perfect and flawless, and the crowd knows it. The crowd is clapping and dancing along as they sing. The duet they are singing is meant to be about a man and a woman, but for Sam, it means more. The words he sings are meant for Eliott. Sam does not know it, but Eliott is singing to him as well.

As they sing their parts of the duet, they casually make eye contact on several lines in the song. They each notice the other looking with deep respect and admiration for each other, sparking feelings within Eliott for the first time. The crowd may not notice the sparks between them, but they notice it. All the crowd hears are the words about a man and woman and not the affection the two are showing to each other on stage. They sing until the song is over, and as soon as it is, the crowd lets them know they want more, either more of their songs or to hear this song again.

As they finish their song, they are so happy by the crowd's response that they take a bow and exit the stage. Regardless of how well they did, they both know someone else is waiting for the next spot, and they know how it is to have a spot at any venue. They exit the stage and make their way back to their table. All the while, the crowd is still shouting and screaming for them to get back on stage. They wave at the crowd and bow to the next performers who are going on stage. Sam and Eliott take a seat at their table.

"WOW! Can you believe this? They love it," Sam expresses to Eliott.

Eliott hears Sam but does not comment as he is listening to the crowd still going wild for them.

"Eliott, did you hear me?"

"Yes, I heard you and this is awesome. They are either very drunk, or they really love our song," Eliott replies.

They continue to sit at their table, listening to the remaining singers for the night before heading home. Their table is full of drinks from all the admirers of their song tonight. They know they cannot drink them all, so they invite Eric over to have a drink with them.

Eliott is confused at first but soon realizes why Sam invited Eric over. It was so he could clean off the table as they left. Eric is not pleased with the outcome of the night, but he did enjoy their song and did not put up a fuss about cleaning up their table.

"Sam, I just want to tell the both of you what an amazing job you guy did tonight. And I am sorry about what happened between us before. Can you forgive me?" Eric confesses to Sam in front of Eliott.

It is Eliott who answers for Sam.

"Can we think about it?"

Sam laughs at Eliott's response to Eric and walks off with Eliott behind him. The two of them continue laughing as they exit through the front door. They are both on an emotional high from their perfect performance earlier and are ready to get home. They both have to get up early tomorrow, and why they feel tonight was a huge success, they know it has to end, for the night anyway.

Sam and Eliott are holding each other up as they are waiting for their car to arrive. They both know they have had too much to drink already for the night. As they hold each other up from falling to the ground, they stop laughing for a split second as they look deeply into each other's eyes. With eyes locked onto one another, they lean their heads in a little closer. As they are about to kiss, their car pulls up, stopping them from moving forward.

"Looks like our car is here," Eliott withdraws his hands from around Sam's waist, releasing him.

Sam shakes his head as if trying to remember where he is and what they are doing. He quickly remembers the night they just had and steps back from Eliott.

"Sorry about that. I forgot we had a car coming. Here, let me get the door for you," Sam quickly responds to Eliott.

"Nothing to be sorry about, I have had an amazing night, and it is all because of you. So, thank you for that. How about you take this car, and I'll get another? I think I should stay at my place tonight so I can get up early tomorrow for work," Eliott expresses appreciation for Sam.

"Are you sure? You can have the bed tonight if you want to stay," Sam questions Eliott's choice to go home for the night.

"Yes, I am sure but thank you for the offer. I will call you tomorrow to schedule more time for more songs if it is okay with you."

"Absolutely. Well, have a good night, and we will talk tomorrow," Sam says his goodbye to Eliott as he pours into the back seat of his ride-share car.

Eliott says goodnight to Sam, shuts the car door, then watches as the car pulls away. Once Eliott is alone on the street, he uses an app to request another car to take him home. As he waits for his car, he seems to find himself thinking about Sam and how well they did tonight. He starts noticing he is developing feelings for Sam, but he is unsure what those feelings are. All he knows is that the feelings he is experiencing put a smile on his face, make his heartbeat faster, and make him warm all over. His thoughts are interrupted when his car arrives to pick him up.

The car stops right in front of Eliott, so he reaches for the door, opens it, and gets in, still with a big smile on his face. Once he closes the door, the car drives off, taking Eliott to his apartment. During the ride home, Eliott thinks about Sam, unsure how to proceed with him and his feelings. Eliott is in deep thought until the car stops in front of his apartment building. Eliott gets out and heads up to his apartment.

As he enters his apartment, the only thing he can think about now is going to bed.

Chapter 5

Spotlight

A couple of months have gone by since Eliott and Sam sang their duet on that faithful Tuesday night. As the months passed, they have been singing the song ever since. They have been asked to sing their duet at every bar in Nashville, giving them any spot they want, as long as they sing the duet. While they have accepted all the invitations, they only agreed to them if they could also have a spot to sing more of their new songs, not just the duet. Each bar agreed to their demands to have them pack their bar with paying customers. Since that first night, they have been working together just about every night writing song after song. As their writing progressed, so did their feelings for each other, but it is not public knowledge.

Performing at all the bars gave Sam and Eliott confidence in their performances and songwriting skills. Eliott, of course, had not told Sam everything about his career of writing songs for other country singers and how well those songs boosted the singers' careers. He was not sure how he would tell him, not since their duet debut. He was afraid Sam would be angry at him for holding back such important information about what he used to do professionally.

Things have been going so well for the both of them, that Eliott started spending most nights at Sam's flat. It was easier for him to stay there so they could continue to write, and Sam's flat was closer to Eliott's work. Even though their feelings have been expressed to each other, Eliott still sleeps on Sam's couch. Feelings or not, this is Eliott's first time having such deep feelings for another person, and he does not want to ruin it by bringing sex into the relationship. He respects Sam and wants to continue working together, particularly since they have been performing well with their music.

Since Eliott has been staying at Sam's flat, he has become more body-positive about himself. He no longer feels ashamed or embarrassed to be undressed in front of Sam. Eliott thinks of it as if he were at the gym and being naked in front of other men in the showers, which was something he had never done before until meeting Sam. Eliott has gained confidence in himself, and to love himself, even if he is different from the man his parents wanted. Even though he was comfortable at the gym and around Sam, he was not yet ready to say anything to his parents about his current situation with Sam.

Tonight, they have a performance at the club where they first performed their duet, The Whiskey Factory where Eric is the bouncer. Jimmy, the open mic coordinator at the bar, called Sam personally and asked if he and Eliott would do him a favor and sing their duet again at the bar. Sales were slowly going down and Jimmy was afraid the bar would go under, and he would lose his job there. He needed a headliner for the evening's performances. Jimmy assured the bar owner that he could pull in a large crowd as long as he could get his biggest act to agree to perform once again in the place that gave them their big break. Same and Eliott agreed. It was in their best interest to return to where it all started for them, not only singing-wise but relationship-wise.

Sam wakes up earlier than Eliott, as usual, and strolls through the living room to the kitchen to make breakfast. Eliott is lying on the couch, naked, with no covers over his smooth body. He is lying there all exposed to the elements and Sam's view. Even though Sam knows their relationship is much different from any other relationship he has been in, he respects Eliott's choice to take things slowly and seriously. Sam fell in love with Eliott before they performed their duet and just knowing Eliott has feelings for him is enough.

As Sam cooks breakfast, Eliott walks into the kitchen naked and kisses Sam on the cheek.

"Good morning, Sam."

"Good morning, Eliott. Are you okay with eggs and pancakes for breakfast?"

"I'm always down for your eggs and pancakes. How much longer until they are ready?" Eliott asks Sam as he wraps his arms around his naked body giving him a big hug before heading off to take a quick shower.

"It's going to be a few minutes," Sam replies.

Once the water is warm, Eliott steps inside the steaming shower and begins to wash off his body with soap. Before he can start washing his hair, Sam walks into the room. Eliott did not mind Sam entering the room until Sam stepped into the shower with him.

"What are you doing?" Eliott asks Sam.

"I thought we could save time and water if we showered together. Is this okay with you?" Sam replies.

Eliott thinks about it for a second before replying to Sam's suggestion.

"Well, if you think it's for the best, then I must agree it is," Eliott expresses to Sam.

The two start by washing themselves with soap and water all over their bodies, while watching the other do the same. They can see the other is just as excited about the new experience they are sharing by the way they both express it, without words, but by the visual aesthetic they both are presenting.

They continue to shower while discussing the songs they will sing tonight at the bar. They know they have to sing their duet, 'Dusty Roads', at least once tonight and want to include two others of their new songs. After much discussion during their shower, they decide on 'Midnight Rains and Heartbreak Trains' and 'Sunset Promises by the Old Creek Bridge'.

"How do you think the crowd will interpret the latter of the two songs?" Eliott asks Sam.

"I think they will love it, and it doesn't matter how they interpret the song. We are the only two who need to know its true meaning and that's good enough for me," Sam replies to Eliott fairly quickly.

Eliott agrees with Sam and finishes his shower. He steps out of the shower and takes a towel to dry off his soaking, wet body. As he is drying off, Sam turns off the water and steps out of the shower. Eliott quickly places his towel into the hamper and walks out of the bathroom, down the hall, and into Sam's room.

Eliott begins to look through the clothes he has brought over to Sam's flat. As he looks through his shirts, he doesn't see anything he wants to wear for the night, so he grabs a t-shirt to throw on for the time being. While Eliott is pulling up his underwear, Sam walks into the room.

"Why are you wearing a t-shirt?" Sam inquires of Eliott.

"I don't have anything here I want to wear tonight. We should go shopping today before the show. We need something flashier for this event. After all, it is the place it all started for us," Eliott suggests to Sam.

Sam acknowledges his suggestion, and following Eliott's lead, he throws on a t-shirt as well. They continue to put on their pants, socks, and shoes before eating breakfast and heading out to shop.

They exit Sam's building and walk down towards 12th Avenue S, where most shops are located. Sam's flat is not far from the area, and it is such a nice day that they walk all the way. They stroll down the street carefree, sharing laughter and jokes. They have no worries between them, and it shows in the way they interact with each other. To many onlookers, they appear to be good friends enjoying the day; however, some begin to question the nature of their relationship. The onlookers wonder if Sam and Elitott are partners in the album they are writing or if they are lovers who happen to write songs. Little do Sam and Eliott know today is when rumors begin to spread around town about them and their relationship.

They finally arrive at 12th Ave S., where the shops are, and enter the first store. They walk through the store looking at shirts, jeans, boots, belts and buckles. They want to be sure they look their best, just in case someone from a recording company is in the crowd tonight. They have been asked to sing their duet by so many bars in town, but not once has an executive from a major record company approached them, and they knew their time was coming. Not finding anything, they decide to head to the next store.

As soon as they exit the store, they are met by a small group of fans. They ask to take photos with them and autographs, asking when their next performance will be. They express their love for the duet, 'Dusty Roads', and want to go to their next show. Sam informs their small group of fans of tonight's show and hopes they will all come. With the fans getting the information they requested, Sam excuses himself and Eliott for having to leave as they are shopping for tonight's show, placing his hand on Eliott's elbow to lead him away from the group.

They continue on their way to the next store, and Eliott is showing signs of anxiety, which Sam notices.

"What's wrong?"

"Nothing. I don't think I'm ready to be in the spotlight with having fans this early in our debut. I get very nervous around groups of strangers. I didn't think our song would be such a hit, but I am fine when I am on stage singing. Maybe it's because they are at a table, and I'm separated from them by the stage. I don't think I can keep shopping today. I will find something to wear at home. Can we return to your place?" Eliott confesses to Sam.

Sam assures Eliott he has nothing to worry about and asks if he wants to take a car back to the flat. Eliott says he does. Sam takes out his phone to call for a car to pick them up at their current location. It arrives only a few minutes later, and Sam puts Eliott in the back seat. Sam tells Eliott he will find them something to wear for tonight and for him to go back to his flat and try to relax. Eliott is not in the mood to argue with Sam, so he agrees to let him shop for them. The car speeds away, leaving Sam on the street to shop for the night.

Sam makes his way through several stores before finding the perfect outfits for them for tonight's event. Now, with the purchases in hand, he steps out of the store and waits for the car he requested to arrive. When it arrives, Sam quickly jumps into the back and sets his bags on the floorboard. The drive back to his flat is very short, so the car stops at his apartment building only a few minutes later. Once stopped, Sam grabs his bags and exits, making his way up to the door of his building.

Sam heads up to his apartment, and as he enters, he finds Eliott asleep on the bed. Presuming he has had time to relax, Sam sets the bags in the living room and walks into his bedroom to wake Eliott. He wants to show him what he bought for them to wear tonight.

"Eliott, are you better now?"

Eliott slowly opens his eyes and looks at Sam with a smile.

"Yes, I am much better now. Did you finish shopping already?"

"I did, and I have something for you to see. So, get up and get your ass into the living room," Sam smirks at Eliott.

Eliott does as asked, crawls out of bed, and makes his way to meet Sam in the living room. He sits next to Sam on the couch in anticipation of what he has picked out for them to wear tonight. Sam slowly pulls out the shirts he bought and hands a dark blue button-up shirt to Eliott.

"I thought this one would be good on you to match your eyes. What do you think?"

Eliott looks at the shirt and then looks over at Sam before answering.

"I love it, Sam. Thank you. What did you buy for you to wear tonight?"

As Eliott patiently waits for Sam to reveal the shirt he got for himself, Sam looks through the other bags until he can find his shirt. Once he finds the right shirt, he pulls it out of the bag and shows it to Eliott. The shirt he picked out for himself is a light gray colored button-up shirt.

"Well, what do you think?" Sam asks for Eliott's thoughts on his shirt.

Eliott looks the shirt over, not saying a word, which makes Sam feel nervous suddenly.

"I think it is perfect for you. I see you got a shirt to match your eyes as well. Is this how we will buy all our clothes now, by the color of your eyes?" Eliott jokes to Sam.

"Ha, ha, ha, Eliott. No, these are not the only colors we will wear from now on. I just thought for tonight we need something to make our presence more noticeable and making our eyes pop is a sure fine way to achieve that goal," Sam replies with a hint of annoyance.

"I was just kidding, Sam. I think these shirts are exactly what we need to make tonight's show even better. I have noticed there are a lot of posts about us on social media and even some posters at bars where we sang. I think tonight's show will be something we will want to remember. If they want to post pictures of us, then the shirts we will wear will be important. You did an amazing job on our outfits for tonight," Eliott reassures Sam.

Realizing they only have an hour to get ready before they head to the bar, they begin to remove the tags off their new clothes and throw them on. They chose to get ready in different rooms to surprise each other with how they looked in their outfits for the night. Once they were both ready, Sam burst into the living room where Eliott got ready.

One looked at the other and they both enjoyed how the other looked. They are both wearing the shirts Sam picked out for them along with new jeans, belt and buckle, and boots. They both looked amazing, and they could feel how the other felt. Without another word, they grabbed their guitars and made their way out of the apartment and down to the street. Their car would be arriving pretty soon, and they were ready to get tonight started.

Sam notices, as they arrive at the bar, that there is a large crowd already outside of it. He can make out some news reporters and cameramen standing beside the reporters. He had no idea the night would be this big of a deal. Then he suddenly started worrying about how Eliott would take all this attention tonight.

"Eliott, are you okay? There is a large crowd outside of the bar for us, I presume. So, how do you want to handle this situation?"

"I think it would be best if they ask any questions, you should answer them. I will be fine once we get inside, so try to give short and simple answers."

"Deal. Remember, tonight is about us and our song, and nothing can take this away from us," Sam reminds Eliott why they are here.

The car stops and Sam is the first to exit, quickly strapping his guitar around his back. Eliott follows suit behind Sam, doing the same thing with his guitar, strapping it around his back. As they stood outside the bar, reporters quickly surrounded them, asking questions. 'How did you come up with your duet' and 'Are you going to be singing anything new tonight?'

Sam takes charge of the questions letting them know of their process of writing 'Dusty Roads' and about how they will sing some new songs tonight. Cameras are flashing all around them, wanting shots of them together and some by themselves. Eliott was happy they got new clothes for the night, and he was sure their appearance would be memorable. He could not wait to tell Sam how amazing he feels at the moment but does anyway. That was until one reporter asked a very unprofessional question.

"Is it true that you are in a relationship with each other? People want to know," Becky from TCM quickly asks Sam.

Sam is shocked at the question he has just been asked and decides not to answer her.

"That will be all folks. We have a show to put on tonight and need to get inside. Thank you all for coming and we hope you enjoy the show," Sam immediately responds to Becky's question, not admitting or denying it, leaving Becky to gather her own opinions about them.

Eliott is obviously not happy about Becky's question, but before he can say anything to her, Sam grabs him by his elbow and leads him away from the crowd of people and into the bar. Once inside, they both can see the club is fully packed tonight, making it hard for them to get to the bar, at first. That is until the people inside recognize who they are and clear a path for them to the bar. Before Sam can order anything, they are both handed shots and beers by the bartender.

"But we didn't order anything yet," Sam tells the bartender.

"It's on the house tonight boys. We also reserved a table for you in the back where you sat last time you were here. Have a great show tonight," the bartender quickly added to her comments.

Sam and Eliott grab their drinks and before they can head to their table towards the back of the bar, Eliott stops in his tracks. He has apparently become nervous about what people will say if they see them sitting alone with each other away from the other tables. He was thinking of Becky's question right before they entered the bar. So he tells Sam he wants another table. Without question, Sam asks the bartender if they could have a different table, one more in the middle of the bar closer to the stage. The bartender is quick to get Eric to get them another table.

They follow Eric to another table closer to the stage. As soon as they are seated, Eric tells them to let him know if they need anything. They nod to Eric as he walks away leaving them to their drinks. Being in the center of the bar, closer to the stage, is a new type of anxiety for Eliott, but he manages his nerves with more shots and beers. They drink until their first spot of the night when Jimmy announces them to the stage.

The announcement that they will perform next throws the crowd into a frenzy. The crowd begins to hoop and holler as Sam and Eliott make their way up and onto the stage. Once they are on stage, Eliott's nerves leave his body. The one thing he knows he can control is how he feels when he sings, and he knows he has nothing to be nervous about. He knows that if anything happens, Sam will be there to cover for him.

Sam begins to strum chords from his guitar letting Eliott know he is ready to start. They sing their duet, 'Dusty Roads', without a hitch, all the while the crowd is loving the song. Cheers and clapping are pouring from everyone at the bar showing much love to them and their song. They exit the stage and make their way back to their table. After sitting down, the crowd quiets as Jimmy announces the next singer to the stage.

Sam and Eliott sit at their table talking to each other and the occasional fan who walks by them. They are having fun drinking more shots and beers. They are immensely enjoying the night, regardless of how it started. They finish the night on a high, with appreciation from their fans after singing their two new songs. They both feel their new songs will become a hit just as much as their duet. Before the night ends, both of them have already forgotten about Becky's question about whether they are in a relationship together. Nothing can take away their fame for the night, not even Becky.

Chapter 6

Crescendo

It has been five months since their performance at the bar that shot their careers into overdrive, and while the show was a super success, it came with some drawbacks. The question Becky asked them back then has come to light, with everyone finding out Sam and Eliott are a couple. They stopped performing at open mic nights, even at the bars requesting them, wanting to avoid being shown in such a negative light because of their relationship. In their opinion, it was nobody's business except their own, but the public didn't see it that way.

The public thinks because their duet was such a hit, they had the right to judge them for being together. They both had many fans who supported their relationship, but they also had other conservative people in country music to oppose their success based on their choice of being together. They both fear the relationship could affect their future in the country music industry. Not only does the public know about their relationship, but Eliott's parents do, too.

Eliott was not thrilled to tell his parents about his sexuality because of an article Becky from TCM put out. He wanted to discuss this with them on his terms when he found the person he wanted to spend the rest of his life with. But he was forced to reveal it to them because of Becky and her opinions of them. He decided to disclose to his parents about him and Sam before they caught wind of it from the papers or some news segment. He went home to let his parents know the truth about his relationship with Sam. While his parents were upset, they eventually came to terms with Eliott's choice of a partner. They both loved Sam and felt he was such a great influence on Eliott. They happily accepted him into the family.

Eliott's parents confessed to Sam that their only son was bullied in school for being such a big music fan, and he ended up with so many emotional issues after he graduated. They thanked Sam for helping him overcome so many of those issues. They noticed just how much Eliott was doing in life after meeting Sam, and they were very thankful for all he had done for him. Eliott did explain to them why he had not come out sooner because he wanted to make sure he came out to them knowing he had the love of his life by his side. While he loves Sam, Eliott informs his parents it is too soon to know if

Sam is the one for his long-term ambitions, but he is happy they got to know him now.

Even though they were still invited to many bars around Nashville, others stopped requesting them when word got out about their relationship. They both knew they had to keep up appearances with the bars that did want them to perform while at the same time trying to get the other bars to see them for what they do, not for who they were to each other. They knew it would be difficult, being in a southern state, but they both knew music was their life and being together was not a lifestyle choice. They wanted people to see that they could not change how they felt about each other because of how the South thought about being homosexual. Their love was as pure as any straight couple, and they were not going to be bullied into submission to please the masses.

Over the past few months, they have had their share of relationship trials. In the beginning, Eliott began to think it would be best for their music careers if they stopped seeing each other. Sam was not happy to hear what Eliott was telling him and pushed for them to stay together. Sam's main point was he didn't want to let the public rule his life regardless of his music career. He debated that if they stuck together during times like they were currently facing, the people would begin to understand how strong their feelings for each other were and eventually learn to accept them for their musical experiences and not their love lives. The only thing Sam truly believed was he did not want to lose Eliott. His love for Eliott was much stronger than his love for country music and losing Eliott would hurt him more than anything in the world.

Sam focused on saving his relationship with Eliott, while Eliott's focus was on how to get the bars who withdrew their support back into their good graces. He repeatedly called every bar owner., letting them know that his relationship with Sam had nothing to do with their music. He continued telling each one about how much they enjoyed performing at their bars and how much of a paying crowd they would bring with them. Eliott was told, over and over again, about how the bar would love to have them back, but they were just so booked these days and had no open spots for them. The bar owners also expressed how they were worried that more gay people would start showing up at their bars because they had a gay couple performing. They feared their conservative bars would become gay bars, which was something they did not want to happen. Their belief in the Bible and their religions were more important to them than a lifestyle gay people 'choose' to live. Eliott continued to assure them that would not happen, as their music was open to everyone to interpret. Their songs were not gay songs but also expressed conservative lifestyles. Their music lyrics did not change because the two singers were a gay couple. Eliott was determined to regain the bars' appreciation of everything they bring to the table, but it would be a long process.

Now, after five months of not performing, they continue to gain invitations to the bars that did accept them for their music, not their lifestyle. Finally, Sam decides it's time to talk Eliott into going back on stage.

"Eliott, it has been five months since we performed at any bar. You do understand many bars are fine with us performing because they love our music, not our relationship. I think it is time for us to start performing again. We have fans who love us and continue to support us in our music endeavors, and we are doing nothing but letting them down by not performing. We owe it to our true fans to accept at least one invitation to perform, and soon," Sam explains to Eliott.

Eliott takes time to go over what Sam has told him before answering.

"Sam, you are right. We have to figure out a way to keep moving forward and show the country music world we are here and, we mean business. I have decided to stop collaborating with the country stars I have worked with in the past unless they begin to show support for us as well. Many of the songs that have made many of them superstars are songs I wrote for them. They know my songs sell records and if they want to stay on top, they will either start supporting us or risk losing their number one songwriter. What do you think?" Eliott outlines his plan for their survival in the country music industry.

Sam can't believe what he is hearing from Eliott. Eliott's songs have been so big to so many artists, that he began to feel Eliott's choice to stop writing songs for them could backfire on him and he was not prepared to have anything happen to Eliott's already established career.

"Eliott, I can't let you do that. If something were to happen and you lost your connections and income, I would never be able to forgive myself for not trying to talk you out of it. You have worked so hard over the years to get to where you are in country music, and while the songs you have written may not be sung by you, those are still your words. I don't want anything to come between you and music. I want you to think about what you are proposing. Ask yourself, how many of your superstar artists will support you and how many could you lose?" Sam relays to Eliott, trying to help him protect his investments in the country music world.

Eliott takes in what Sam is expressing to him but on the other hand, he does not care. He is upset about how people are treated, not only in the country music industry but also in life. He hates the fact everyone has to conform to religious beliefs to succeed in life. Eliott thinks back to a lesson from college about US History and the Bill of Rights. All he can think about is the preamble of the Declaration of Independence, 'We hold these truths to be self-evident, that all men are created equal, that they are endowed by their Creator with certain unalienable Rights, that among those are Life, Liberty and the pursuit of Happiness', and how those words which grant everyone the same rights, condemns many people without those rights promised to them by the Constitution of the United States (1787). He felt it was his duty to either make the country music industry respect his rights or take them away from the superstars he had written songs for.

"I have made my decision. This is exactly what I will propose to my clients. If they want me to continue to write chart toppers for them, then they will need to show support for what we can contribute to country music. I have been gay my entire life but never felt the need to express it until now. Their songs were written by a gay man, songs that shot them into superstardom, and it's time the world knew it. Our songs are just as good and just because we are gay men in a relationship, it would not matter to the industry since I have been providing songs based on my feelings for so long now for other artists to sing. Those are my words based on my feelings, so just because we are together, it should not negate the value of our words in a song. If they can make it big off my feelings, then so can we," Eliott defends his decision.

Sam doesn't have to think about what Eliott told him before exclaiming,

"This is exactly why I love you so much! You are willing to throw away everything you have been doing to defend your feelings and love for not only me but for the country music industry. You make me so proud, but only if you are completely sure this is something you want to do," Sam questions Eliott, once more for clarity.

Eliott confirms with Sam his decision has already been made and he will be contracting his clients to inform them of his decision. Even though he wrote the songs for other singers to sing, he owns the rights to each song. They will either back them or lose some of their most popular songs on their albums.

It did not take Eliott long to get every client on board with his requests. It only took another two weeks before word got out about how so many superstars in country music began showing support for Sam and Eliott's relationship and their songs. Once word got out, it did not take long for the bars that once restricted their presence at their establishments to call them to invite them back to their bars to sing. Their world was beginning to look up once again.

Chapter 7

Dissonance

It has been a month since Eliott's clients began showing support for his and Sam's relationship and their music. Things have been going well for them, from being interviewed on TCM (Television for Country Music) to appearing on late-night shows on other networks. Their lives were exactly where they wanted them to be. Their love for each other and country music was obvious to everyone who saw their shows. Everyone except certain religious groups.

It all started a few months back when they were performing at a new bar in New York City. When Sam and Eliott arrived at the venue, they had their usual supportive groups outside whooping and hollering, but there was also a new group. The new group was a small group of religious members from a country church from Texas. They held up signs of their disapproval of any gay couple who not only was in the country music industry but also any gay couple at all. Their belief was about how music was meant for spiritual members of Christ and other biblical beliefs. Those beliefs were based on a

Bible verse, Leviticus 20 – 13, "If a man lies with a man as with a woman, they have committed an abomination; the two of them shall be put to death; their blood is upon them." While this verse means something to the group, it means nothing to Sam and Eliott. They are both Christians but have different meanings of the verse, so they walk past the group into the venue to enjoy their show for the night.

They thought they handled the situation with pride by ignoring the protestors and thought nothing more about it. A few months went by and the same religious group was on TCM speaking about Sam and Eliott. They began talking about how being a homosexual was a sin and that anyone who listened to their music or showed support for the singers was committing a sin as well. Derek Hall, the group's leader, is a veteran country music singer in his early fifties. He is rugged with a commanding presence and deep-set blue eyes. Derek used to support Sam and Eliott's music until they came out as a couple. His conservative views on life challenge him with the changing norms of the country music industry, and he is unafraid to speak his mind.

As Derek continues speaking about the singers, he says something that catches Sam and Eliott's attention.

"While Sam and Eliott's songs may sound great to the average person, everyone in country music knows their music is stolen from other artists. The two of them may have been able to come up with a couple of words for their songs, but they stole the music from artists who trusted Eliott. You see, Eliott used to write songs for many of the superstars we have today, but before he quit writing for those singers, he secretly was recording the songs to use later. He thought if he and Sam put out their music first, no one would ever know." Derek tells the host of the TCM show who is interviewing him.

Sam gazes at Eliott in shock. He hopes Derek is lying about Eliott, but it sounds as if it could be true. Eliott turns to look at Sam as he turns the television down.

"What's the matter, Sam? You know he is lying, don't you?"

"Of course, I do. I know we came up with the music together, making it original," Sam quickly responds to Eliott.

"Good, because we need to get ahead of this before people start believing him. I'm sure this is not as bad as it seems. Luckily, I have an attorney I will contact later today to see what we can do about Derek Hall," Eliott tells Sam to ease his fears.

As the day continued, Sam and Eliott's phones rang non-stop from friends and family as word got out about what Derek said on national television. Their friends and family gave them as much support as they needed to help them navigate through this situation. Some gave them names and numbers of lawyers they knew, while others told them they didn't believe a word Derek said and others wouldn't either. They all said that only time would tell, and to let it fade away.

Later in the day, Eliott scheduled a meeting with his attorney, Laura Davenport. Laura has been a lawyer in Nashville for over fifteen years and has represented many local country singers and recording labels. She has a proven track record for defending her clients with the full force of the law. Laura has a record of winning ninety-five percent of all her cases. She is exactly what is needed right now.

Sam and Eliott get ready for their meeting with Laura, which is in an hour. Her office is in downtown Nashville and only a ten-minute walk from Sam's flat, so they know they have some time to talk before they have to leave.

"Sam, are you worried about any of this? Do you think we will be okay? I know I never stole anyone's music, especially from someone I have worked with previously. You remember my ex-boyfriend, the one I told you about the night we met at Dawn Café? Well, I am sure this is all his work. I bet he is the one who told Derek those things hoping he can become relevant again since he has fallen off the charts."

"Eliott, I know you are telling the truth, and I am sure none of your previous clients ever said you stole their music, except maybe him. Have you spoken to any of your former clients yet? Have any of them contacted you to say it wasn't them?"

"I have heard from a couple of them, and they assured me they never would have said anything like that to Derek or anyone else. Some clients have been suggested as possible sources for the comment, but that's only because they haven't achieved significant success yet. They seemed frustrated because they hoped my songwriting skills would help elevate their careers. I have not reached out to them, nor them to me, but they do not make me nervous. I still bet my money on my ex."

"Well, make sure you let Laura know what your clients have told you about the others so she can investigate them. It sounds petty of them to do something like this to try and make you come back to write for them, but the music industry is cutthroat, so anything is possible. Be sure you let Laura know more about your ex even though you haven't told me his name."

They ended their conversation on that note, and once they were ready, they left Sam's building and headed down the street to Laura's office. Walking along the streets of Nashville, they notice people pointing at them and softly speaking to each other. Sam assumes they either watched the TCM interview with Derek or have seen something on social media. Sam and Eliott ignore the pointing and whispering on the streets but walk a little faster.

As soon as they arrive at Laura's office building, they enter and go to the concierge's desk to let Laura know they are there. While the concierge is making the call to Laura, Sam and Eliott sit in the lobby of the large building. They sit next to each other, not worried about anyone seeing them together. The fact is, they hope people will see them together, showing no fear from Derek's words. They know they have to stand strong in the face of the public if they want to be presumed innocent.

"Laura will see you now. Please take the elevator up to the fourteenth floor. She will be waiting for you," the concierge directed Sam and Eliott toward the elevators in the center of the building.

Once inside the elevator, the doors closed, and it began making its way up to the fourteenth floor. When the elevator stopped, the doors opened, and standing right in front of the elevator was Laura. She greets them both and instructs them to follow her to her office.

Laura leads them down a few hallways until they reach her office. She holds her door open for Sam and Eliott to enter first. She follows, closing her office door behind her.

Laura asks Sam and Eliott to have a seat in the two large empty chairs that are right in front of her desk. As they take their seats, Laura walks around her desk and sits in her oversized executive chair. Laura looks very small to them both once she is seated in the chair, but they try not to stare at her.

"So, Eliott, you have filled me in on some bits for this meeting, so let's get started. I have carefully reviewed Derek Hall's interview on TCM. While he repulses me, there may be some legal action you can take against him, such as a defamation lawsuit. That is the action taken against someone who tells others false information about someone with no evidence to support his claim. Now, to do this, we will need to make sure he does not have any evidence about you stealing other artists' music. That brings me to another question. Who do you think could have said something like that to Derek? Do you have any enemies?" Laura begins to explain the steps she believes will best suit them moving forward.

"Thank you, Laura, for seeing us. Yes, I have spoken to a couple of my previous clients who all have said they believe it could be one, or two, of my most recent clients who were expecting my songs to boost their careers to the next level. But I have been thinking about it, and I think it could be my ex-boyfriend, Chad. When I moved to Nashville, I met Chad at a bar and we hit it off. We started dating shortly after we met. He was my first actual boyfriend to be honest. He had done his research on me, via the internet. He found out about how I was found by some small talent managers when I was in high school. He did more research and found out I was writing songs for other artists, which at the time I did not know he knew so much about me. I began writing songs for him on the side and not covering myself as the songwriter for the music he put out because we were serious, or so I thought. It was not long after he became a hit he left me and never spoke to me again. If anyone is behind all of these rumors, I would suspect him first," Eliott tells Laura before he gives her the names of any possible clients.

Laura takes notes on everything Eliott is telling her. Once he is finished, she turns her attention to Sam.

"Sam, it's so nice to meet you. I have heard your and Eliott's songs, and I love them. I have to ask, and this may be difficult for you, but I need to know the truth. This will not be a jab at you or me trying to catch you lying, but it will come up later if it goes to court. We need to cover all the bases. Do you understand?" Laura asks Sam, looking him straight in the eyes.

Sam leans forward in his seat and begins to sweat. He has no clue what Laura will ask him, but he knows he has nothing to hide.

"I understand completely. I have nothing to hide, and you will only get the truth from me, especially if it's anything to do with Eliott," Sam assures Laura.

"Okay, then, I hate to ask this, but I must. Since working with Eliott, have you noticed anything unusual with his music writing? Like, during any of your writing sessions, have you ever heard him using any other artists' music to the words you both created?"

"Absolutely not! Everything we have written has been an original song with each of us putting our own spin to the songs."

"Thank you. Now, are you and Eliott in a committed relationship?"

"What does that have to do with Eliott stealing music?" Sam quickly asks Laura.

"Well, Derek Hall is a conservative man with very conservative views. It could come up. I know you both have not confirmed nor denied being a couple, but if you are in a committed relationship, it could show why you may have a reason to lie for Eliott," Laura explains the question more to them both.

"Well, we have never really talked about whether or not we are committed to each other, but we are in a relationship with each other in many ways. We are dating, and we are also committed to writing new music together. But that does not give me a reason to lie for Eliott. I have no reason to lie for him because nothing Derek said on TV was true," Sam passionately replies to Laura.

Laura takes notes on what Sam is telling her, the same way she did when Eliott was speaking to her. She can tell she hit a nerve with Sam when he was talking about him and Eliott being committed to each other. She needs to probe deeper to be sure Sam is not hiding anything from her that could harm Eliott in the future.

"Thank you, Sam, for your honesty. Now, I have another question for you. Since you and Eliott have been in a relationship, have you been with anyone besides Eliott?"

"Why is it whenever something is said about a gay couple, they assume one of them is cheating on the other? As if it is the standard of gay relationships. The answer is no! I have not been with anyone since we started dating. And if you must know, Eliott and I have not been together sexually. Does that answer your question?"

"Sam, Laura is just doing her job. These things could be asked if we have to go to court, and she doesn't want to be blindsided in court by something we leave out. It's okay, I promise." Eliott tries to relax Sam.

Sam slows his breathing and composes himself before speaking to Laura.

"I'm sorry for my outburst, Laura. It drives me crazy because so many people think all gay relationships are open relationships, which is not true. Our relationship is just as real as a straight couple. We are committed to each other, and that is all."

"I completely understand what you mean. As Eliott said, I don't want to be caught off guard if this goes to court. We prefer to resolve this matter outside of court. Is there anything else either one of you can think of that I may need to know before beginning fact-finding for this case?" Laura asks them one last time.

"No, I can't think of anything off the top of my head, but if we do think of anything, you will be the first to know. Thank you, Laura, for agreeing to take my case," Eliott expresses to Laura.

Eliott and Sam thank Laura again as they leave her office. She assures them that she will do everything she can to find out who told Derek those lies, if anyone actually did. She explains that it could all be a ruse created by Derek to draw attention to himself. His career has been declining for years, so this might be his attempt to regain relevance in today's country music scene. They know she would get to the truth one way or another, and that is all they want, for the truth to come out.

Sam and Eliott make their way through the hallways until they reach the elevators. As soon as they enter the elevator, the door closes, and they descend to the first floor. When they exit the elevator and turn towards the entrance of the building, they can see a crowd gathered out front of the building. At first, they were not sure who they were there for, but they had no idea they were there for them. Someone noticed them entering an attorney's office and leaked it to the press. Heads held high, Sam and Eliott walked out of the front door as calmly as they did when they arrived until they were outside.

As soon as they exited the building, the crowd outside the entrance of Laura's office building began yelling out questions for them.

"Eliott, did you steal your music from your clients?"

"Sam, when did you start cheating on Eliott and why?"

"Are you two dating in real life, or is your relationship all fake to get other gays to like your music?"

At first, Eliott is confused by the questions they are shouting at them. He is unaware of the source of their information, but it appears to be inaccurate. Eliott begins to wonder if these accusations are from Derek Hall himself. Then he wonders what Derek thought he could gain from these lies. Eliott looks at Sam with an expression of, "Get me out of here!" Sam notices Eliott's look and grabs his hand to lead him out of the crowd to the car waiting for them. He requested the car without Eliott noticing when he saw the crowd standing outside Laura's building when they exited the elevator.

After Sam and Eliott retreated into the car and were on their way back to Sam's flat, Eliott squeezed Sam's hand hard. He was not ready to face the media, especially when they asked about things that had nothing to do with country music or their personal lives. He didn't know what to expect, not really, when he and Sam announced their relationship, but he didn't think it would be this difficult. Eliott struggled to understand why people were upset about their relationship. He felt, deep down, that he may have to speak about him being gay, but he never expected it to cause such a scandal about not only the lies about him stealing music from a client but also infidelity rumors about Sam. He needs Sam to know he does not believe anything the reporters are saying.

"Sam, are you okay?"

Sam softly looks into Eliott's eyes and knows he can not lie to him.

"I'm so sorry, Eliott. I never meant for any of this to hurt you, much less come out at all. There is something I need to tell you, but I want you to know how much I love you!"

Eliott unclenches his hand from Sam's and draws it quickly back to his lap. He was caught off guard by the reporters, but even so more by Sam's choice of words just now.

"What are you talking about, Sam? Are you saying there is some truth to what the reporters were asking me about you?" Eliott asks Sam with shock in his voice.

Sam takes a moment to think about how he wants to answer Eliott's question. He knows what he is about to tell him will hurt him, but it is not his intention.

"I am not sure how to say this, but I have to tell you something. Before you and I became serious with each other, I may have had a sexual one-night stand. It was after one of our shows and you wanted to go home. I said I was going home too, but I didn't. I went back inside the bar and had a few more drinks. You have to understand we were doing so well, and things were getting so good for us. I didn't want the night to end. I saw Eric at the door when I was leaving. He hit me up again, wanting to hook up for the night. I agreed. I am so sorry, Eliott. Can you ever forgive me?" Sam comes clean with his indiscretion from so long ago.

After Eliott hears what Sam has just told him, he is not upset. Deep down, he felt that Sam and Eric may have messed around at one point or another. He knew there was something up between them when Sam asked Eric over to their table that night to clear off the table. Eliott felt that Sam having Eric clear off the table was a bit overboard, but he let it go. Eliott never thought about that night again until tonight.

Chapter 8

Fortissimo

It has been a couple of days since the incident of the crowd of reporters standing outside of Laura's office building. That was the day Sam confessed to having a one-night stand with Eric, the bouncer at the Whiskey Factory, the bar that put their music on the map. Eliott may have thought Sam and Eric had something at one point or another, but he did not expect Sam to admit it. Eliott was surprised by the questions the reporters asked him. They had nothing to do with stolen music. That is what Derek Hall had been spewing all over social media. Eliott needed time to think about how he wanted to proceed, not only with his relationship with Sam but also with their music career.

Sam has not been out of his flat for several days and called Eliott at least once every day. Eliott never answered his calls or returned them. Sam feared that not only his career with Eliott was in jeopardy but also their relationship. He knew what he had told Eliott about him and Eric was a lot of information. Sam felt Eliott would come to his senses and forgive him even though Sam didn't feel he needed forgiveness. When he and Eric hooked up, he and Eliott were not a thing; they were just writers creating music together. Sam wasn't giving up on Eliott, and he felt Eliott was not giving up on him either. Finally, after three days, Eliott returns Sam's calls.

"Sam, I'm sorry I have not been returning your calls, but this has been a great deal for me to handle. I may have been selfish in avoiding you, but I needed time to think. I hope you have also had time to think about everything. I don't want what we have to end. It's okay that you and Eric hooked up since we weren't together then. It only hurt me because I had to learn about you two from a reporter. I hope you understand," Eliott expresses to Sam.

"Eliott, I am so sorry about all of this. I was not thinking that night I hooked up with Eric. He was just there at the time, and I was thinking with my dick and not my brain. I know that is not an excuse, and I can only say how sorry I am about that night. I never thought my one-night stand could turn into such a scandal with everything we have going on right now. I hope we are okay and will get through this together," Sam expresses to Eliott, hoping to keep their personal and working relationship intact.

While Eliott is speaking to Sam, their call is interrupted by a call from Clara Jameson. Clara has been Eliott's music producer for several years. She has an amazing track record with other artists and is very progressive. Clara is sharp, insightful, and nurturing to her clients in country music. Over the past year, she has been a mentor to Eliott and Sam ever since they started collaborating. Even though she has had Eliott as a client for years, she was open to accepting Eliott and Sam together. Clara has been telling Eliott for years that he needed to stop writing songs for other artists and has always encouraged him to write songs for himself.

"Sam, I have to let you go for now. Clara is calling, and I need to speak with her," Eliott explains to Sam.

Sam understood how important it was for Eliott to speak with Clara and let their call end. He began to feel better about their relationship and current situation when he hung up.

"Clara, thank you for calling me back. What do you suggest we do now? We need some ideas of how Sam and I can get this all past us," Eliott asks Clara with a hint of desperation.

"Frankly, Eliott, I do have an idea. I am not sure if you would be open to it, but I know Sam will be," Clara begins telling Eliott.

"Well, don't hold back now. We need something to get our music back on track. These distractions from Derek Hall and whoever Sam slept with are putting the wrong attention on us. I never stole anyone's music, and Sam didn't cheat on me. Everything has been blown out of proportion. So, what do you have in mind?" Eliott quickly responds to Clara.

"I think you and Sam need to have a large concert, not just any concert, but THE concert of the year. It should be an all-inclusive concert event. It should be a concert for everyone, gay, straight, bi-sexual, trans-sexual, Baptist, Methodist, Catholic, Republican, and Democrat. Everyone should be invited to this concert so you and Sam can show everyone what your music is all about. It's not about two gay men loving each other, or it could be, but more about how the lyrics and music touch the people who listen to the music. Let them feel the words and affection you are sending them as individual people. What do you think about that? Do you think Sam will be on board?" Clara reveals her plan to get them back where they were before all the Derek Hall rumors started.

"WOW! That is one huge plan you have for us. Are you sure we are ready for something like that? We have only been playing at local bars and had a few TV interviews. Do you think we are ready for a large concert?" Eliott asks Clara out of fear for himself and his performance.

"It does not matter if I think you are both ready for this, it all comes down to if you feel you are ready. Do you think you can handle it?" Clara asks Eliott. "Because I believe you both have it in you to do this."

Eliott does not reply to Clara at first. He is sitting there with his phone to his ear, thinking about a large crowd who could be at a concert to see him and Sam perform. He is not sure how he should reply to Clara.

"Can I speak to Sam before I commit to anything? It is a decision we should make together. Don't you agree?" Eliott nervously responds to Clara's suggestion.

"Yes, speak to Sam and let me know. If you both agree with this plan, let me know so I can begin to make the preparations for the concert," Clara relays to Eliott before she ends their call.

While Eliott is terrified of having a large concert for him and Sam to perform their music, he believes it is the only way to get the focus away from any rumors from Derek Hall or Sam's possible indiscretion and back on to their music. He may not like the fact that Clara could be right, but he knew she was right. He needs to talk to Sam to get his opinion on this subject.

Eliott picks up his phone and presses the buttons to call Sam. As the phone rings, Eliott has mixed emotions about it all. On the one hand, he feels Clara is right about having a large concert and including everyone. However, he is concerned about his ability to perform before such a large audience. Eliott only has a minute to think about those things before Sam answers the call.

"Eliott, what did Clara say?"

"Sam, I need to come over if it's okay. Clara did give me some thoughts on what she thinks should happen next, but I think it would be best if we spoke about it in person and not over the phone," Eliott tells Sam without answering his question right off the bat.

Sam agrees to allow Eliott to come over to discuss what Clara told him, but when the call ends, Sam feels nervous. He was afraid Clara, being Eliott's music producer for so many years, told Eliott to leave him and start over. He doesn't know what to expect when Eliott comes over, but he at least wants to be sure his flat looks good. Sam begins frantically cleaning his apartment. He ran around picking up anything that did not belong on the floor or table, like clothes, cups, dishes, and even empty pizza boxes. Sam was not ready for Eliott to see how well he had been doing since the other night. He didn't want Eliott to see he had been a hot mess without him. As soon as Sam finishes cleaning the apartment, he hears the buzzer to the flat. It is Eliott down at the entrance doors.

Sam buzzes Eliott in, and as he makes his way up to his apartment, Sam throws things anywhere he can find to hide the evidence of his sadness. Soon, there is a knock at his door. It's Eliott.

"Hey, Eliott, please come in. I was surprised when you asked to come over. I guess Clara had some things to tell you that you wanted to say in person, but before you tell me, I must say again how sorry I am for sleeping with Eric. He meant nothing to me. Please don't end everything we have together because of one mistake I made," Sam pleads with Eliott before he can even come through the door.

"May I come in?" Eliott asks Sam without acknowledging the other comments he just made.

Sam doesn't say a word but instead stands aside and lets Eliott enter his apartment. He closes the door behind Eliott. He lets him get seated on the couch and takes a seat on the chair across from him.

"Sam, Clara has an idea I think you will like, but I have some reservations about it. Clara thinks we should have a large concert and invite anyone of any background and political backing. Now, when I say concert, I am not talking about just another night at the bar like we have been doing, but a full-blown concert at a large venue. She thinks we have to make people remember why they love our music and our lyrics. None of this has anything to do with us splitting up, which I don't want either. I love you, and I know what you did was not done intentionally to hurt me. I know it was before we even considered ourselves in a committed relationship. I respect you, Sam. I am sorry I have dragged you into my drama with Derek Hall. I never thought any of my past clients would ever accuse me of stealing their music. Laura has been working on that. She found out who said those things. She got them to drop all charges since we have time stamps on all of our music that predated anything they came up with. So that has been settled," Eliott explains to Sam with hesitation.

"But?" Sam replies, noticing Eliott's reservations.

"But nothing. I swear. I only needed time to think about how I would process all these negative responses from previous fans. I never thought being in the spotlight would be so hard, but I am learning it is harder than I ever imagined. Being hit with those questions about you and Eric took me by surprise. I didn't know how to handle it, but I knew it was not your fault. I am worried about how things will be between us if we have to defend ourselves from social media forever. What did we do that was any different from any other country singers? We began collaborating together and eventually fell in love. Our music should not be disliked because of our feelings for each other. Our words are true and can mean anything to anyone who listens to our songs," Eliott reassures Sam's negative thoughts.

"Are you serious? You are not mad at me because of Eric?"

"No, I am not upset about you and Eric hooking up. You were free to do whatever you wanted until we became an actual couple, but then you did not have the right to do whatever you wanted. I understand that our relationship may be different from others, but since you are only my second boyfriend, I want to take things slow. I wondered if my choice of not sleeping with you could drive you to sleep with other people. But I never thought you would or did. Again, not after we became a couple," Eliott tells Sam with love in his voice and eyes.

After speaking about Clara's idea and agreeing to have a concert, they begin to think about where the concert should be and when they should have it. They discussed many different large venues, but not stadium large, for their concert. They decided to check on the size of the amphitheater in Nashville and how many people it could hold. When they find out it can hold up to 6,800 people, Sam and Eliott decide to let Clara know it is where they want to have their concert. With the location of their concert picked, they need to find out when it will be available.

Eliott tells Sam, "Clara can figure all this out and make the arrangements for us. I will tell her what we want and see what she can do."

Eliott calls Clara and tells her that he and Sam settled on a location for the concert. Eliott tells her that they need her to check the venue's availability. Clara agreed to contact the venue to set a date for Eliott and Sam's concert and told Eliott she would get back to him as soon as she confirmed things with the amphitheater. Eliott hung up and explained to Sam that Clara would be booking their concert venue and letting them know when it would be.

Now, with Clara taking charge of contacting the venue and trying to confirm a date for Sam and Eliott's concert, they decided to take a break from going out for a while. They choose to spend more time together to get to know each other even more.

A few months go by without hearing from Clara, and Sam asks Eliott to contact her. He wants to make sure she is truly supporting them and that her convictions have not changed. Eliott assures Sam that Clara has their best interests in mind.

"This concert has to be amazing. We need to show the people we have nothing but love in our hearts and that will be portrayed through our music. We have to write new songs to show our fans exactly what we want them to take from our songs. Love. That is what we have for each other and everyone else. We need to show the country music industry that it is not only for straight men. There are all types of gay men, including gay men who love country music. But I also believe our music needs to extend past us being gay. It needs to exude love for all sexual preferences. We have to find a way to ensure straight men can feel the love that we have for each other in a way they can show to their girlfriends or wives," Eliott reiterates to Sam.

For the next two weeks, Sam and Eliott discuss how they grew up and how they were treated by friends and family. They want to put their hardships into lyrics anyone can relate to. During one of their late-night talks, they both felt the other had not only had to deal with being gay but also about just being different. As Eliott was not out as a child or a teenager, coming out as a young adult, he was called names in school. His schoolmates called him a queer, fag, or just gay all the time. He never understood why they called him those names because he never knew what those words meant. The town he grew up in was not large, and it had no gay bars or clubs in it or any gay people he knew about. He always wondered where those kids got those words from and how they knew what they meant. He assumed those kids learned those words from their parents. Eliott's parents never allowed him to be exposed to things like that. He was restricted to the internet or social clubs by his parents, so his knowledge of the LGBTQ+ world was limited, to say the least.

Sam, on the other hand, was already an out and proud adult when Eliott met him that fateful night at The Whiskey Factory. During their discussions that night, Eliott heard stories of how Sam was treated before and after he came out of the closet. He was treated the same as Eliott before he came out by other classmates. But he was treated even worse after coming out. Sam endured daily beatings from classmates during school, after school, and on weekends. He had very few friends growing up because of how he was perceived by classmates, even though he lived in Austin, Texas, which had a fairly large LGBTQ+ community. Eliott assumed because he grew up in a town that had gay people and even gay bars, he would have been accepted by his classmates and family. That wasn't the case. That led them both to understand it does not matter where or how you are raised, people who are different will be told they are different most of their lives. This also refers to being a tall girl or a very short boy, the same thing between rich and poor kids. Everyone is treated differently. Sam and Eliott want to let their fans know they have had enough of how people are treated differently for any reason.

As they swapped stories about growing up and coming out, they realized that regardless of how and where they were raised, they were treated the same way. So, they picked something from the other one's stories to come up with lyrics everyone could relate to, not only the LGBTQ+ community.

Chapter 9

The Great Performance

Eliott and Sam continue to write new songs incorporating their lives growing up. The moments they were both treated poorly by friends and family while being raised in different circumstances. They had their ups and downs, but in the end, their lives were not so different. Once they were satisfied with the words of their songs, they moved on to the notes and rhythm of the music to match the intro, verse, pre-chorus, chorus, and bridge of their songs. They worked for several days before hearing from Clara about their actual concert date and venue.

Finally, Clara called Eliott with the final date and venue for their largest performance to date, a large venue with at least 6,800 fans to listen to their songs. Clara tells Eliott that they don't have to worry about finding the venue because she researched and checked to make sure they could fill the place with no problems.

"Eliott, I have found the perfect place for you and Sam to have this concert. It will be the largest place you have ever performed. Will you both be able to perform in such a large venue for the first time?" Clara asks Eliott.

Eliott looks over at Sam after asking Clara to hold on for a moment and asks Sam the same question Clara just asked him.

"Sam, Clara wants to be sure we are good for performing in a tremendously large venue. You know, with nerves and all. What do you think?"

"What do I think? You tell her we are ready for any venue she can find, big or small. We have been waiting our entire lives for this moment and will not mess it up," Sam replies to Eliott.

Eliott gets back to Clara on the phone and relays what Sam has just told him, word for word. They chat for a few minutes before Eliott hangs up with her. After their call, Eliott puts his phone back inside his pocket and smiles at Sam.

"Do you genuinely think we will be ready? You remember that I have never performed in front of a large crowd, so this will be new for me. Honestly, I am a little nervous about this concert," Eliott confesses to Sam.

Sam stands up from the couch, walks over to Eliott, opens his arms, and hugs Eliott in a tight bear hug.

"Eliott, you have nothing to worry about. I will be with you the entire time. All you have to do is look at me until you are comfortable enough to look at the crowd. Then, you can do anything you put your mind to. We will be fine, trust me," Sam tries to comfort Eliott's nerves.

Eliott feels better with Sam's words and relaxes because Sam has never pointed him in the wrong direction. Eliott is tired from writing songs all day, and after hearing Clara has found a venue for them to play in, he is ready for some sleep.

"Sam, if it's okay with you, I think I need to go home to sleep tonight. Would you like to join me?" Eliott casually asks Sam.

Sam is uncertain about Eliott's offer but chooses to accept it. Sam has only been to Eliott's place a couple of times over the years because they usually write songs at Sam's place, and he has never questioned why. So, to Sam, it's an opportunity to get to know Eliott even more.

They leave and head over to Eliott's place for the night. They walked out of Sam's building, and a car was already waiting for them. It was clear to Sam that Eliott had requested the car to go to his place for the night. Eliott opens the door to the back seat and allows Sam to enter first. Once Sam is seated, Eliott climbs into the back seat and closes the door. When the door closes, Eliott takes Sam's hand and places it on his lap.

The car moves towards Eliott's apartment, or so Sam thinks, but it stops after a few minutes.

They are in front of The Whiskey Factory, the bar that gave them notoriety in the country music industry. Sam is surprised that Eliott requested a car to take them to a bar instead of going to his place.

"Eliott, what are we doing here? I thought we were going to your place to go to bed and get some sleep," Sam inquires of Eliott.

Eliott gives Sam a cute smile and opens the car door after the car stops. When Eliott is out of the car, he reaches into the car and takes Sam's hand to help him out of the backseat. Sam, of course, takes hold of Eliott's hand and steps out of the car. Eliott leads them towards the door where Eric, the doorman at the bar who had a crush on Sam, is standing. As they make their way to the entrance of The Whiskey Factory, Eric can't do anything except watch as Eliott leads Sam into the bar, hand-in-hand.

"What are you doing, Eliott?" Sam inquires.

"What do you mean? I want to take you out to celebrate the fact we now have a venue for our first large concert. Is that okay with you?" Eliott lets Sam in on his plans for the night.

"Thank you. But this is so unexpected. Usually, when you say you are tired and want to go to bed, you mean it. Tonight, has caught me off guard for the first time since I met you. I will follow your direction for the night if you are fine with it," Sam tells Eliott.

Eliott takes a minute and looks at Sam, giving him a suggestive look of, 'I have the night.' Sam decides to give himself wholly to Eliott. Sam can feel Eliott will never hurt him, so he will relax and enjoy the night. Sam is ready to let their night begin.

Once inside The Whiskey Factory, Eliott leads them to their regular table. They take their seats at the table before anyone notices who they are. They are grateful that they are not recognized by the regulars at the bar. Eliott calls a waitress over to place an order for them.

"Excuse me, can we order some drinks, please?" Eliott asks the closest waitress walking by.

"Sorry, your table is not in my area, but I will find your waitress and let her know you are ready to order," the unsuspecting waitress replies until she notices who they are.

"Are you Sam and Eliott?" the unknown waitress asks Eliott.

"If I say we are, would you get our drinks?" Eliott quickly asks the waitress.

"Of course, I would," she replies.

"Then, no, we are not Sam and Eliott. Can you get our actual waitress please?" Eliott quickly responds to her.

"Sorry, you just look like them…"

"We are not them, so please get our waitress. We are ready to order," Sam quickly chimes in taking the lead from Eliott.

"Rude! Fine, I will find the waitress for your table," the waitress replies to Sam and walks off quickly and upset.

"I'm sorry, Eliott. I also didn't how she wanted to take our orders because of who we were and not because we were just thirsty. I hope I did not upset you," Sam explains to Eliott.

"Sam, you are perfectly fine. I was going to say the same thing to her. You can't do anything to mess this night up, so just be ready to enjoy the night," Eliott reassures Sam with an ominous look.

As Sam notices the look on Eliott's face, one he has never seen before, he is unsure of what Eliott has in store for them for tonight. Sam decides to sit back and let Eliott handle the remainder of the night at The Whiskey Factory. Sam has been waiting for Eliott to show his 'take charge' side and does not want to do anything to interrupt Eliott's mood before going home with him for the first time.

It takes several minutes before the waitress assigned to their table shows up. She doesn't ask who they are before taking their order.

"Hello fellas, my name is Natasha. I am your server for the night. What can I get for you guys?" Natasha asks them.

"Nice to meet you, Natasha. We are Sam and Eliott. We want two Jager bombs and two Coors lights. Can you make that happen?" Eliott quickly responds to Natasha.

"Yes sir, I will be right back," Natasha replies as she walks towards the bar.

While Natasha is gone, Eliott initiates a questionable sexual conversation with Sam.

"So, Sam, how many men have you been with?"

Sam takes a few minutes before he answers Eliott's question.

"Why are you asking me that, Eliott? It does not seem like the right place to discuss this, don't you agree?" Sam responds.

"Sorry, Sam. I was trying to make conversation while we waited for Natasha. I didn't mean to cause a stir in you. We can talk about something else if you like," Eliott tells Sam with no regrets in his earlier question.

"No, it's fine. I knew this question would come up at some point in our relationship. Honestly, I don't believe this is the best night to discuss my sexual history, but I am willing to answer all your questions at a later date. Tonight is supposed to be a fun night, and I don't think talking about past sexual experiences will be a fun topic to talk about. I hope you understand," Sam quickly expresses to Eliott.

Before Eliott can reply to Sam, Natasha shows up with their beers and shots.

"Excuse me, gentleman, I have your drinks," Natasha tells Sam and Eliott.

Natasha sets their drinks down as Sam thanks her. Eliott also thanks Natasha before she walks away, leaving the two to talk together. Of course, Eliott does not revisit his previous conversation with Sam, he moves on to talk about their upcoming concert.

"So, Sam, how do you think we will do at the concert? Do you think it will be enough to stop people from talking about the rumors of me stealing my clients' songs?" Eliott inquisitively asks Sam.

"Don't worry about what your clients are saying. You and I both know we came up with our songs on our own. They have nothing backing up their stories. We will come out victorious from our concert, trust me," Sam reassures Eliott.

Sam and Eliott continue to enjoy their night at The Whiskey Factory before going home to Eliott's place. They leave the bar and take a car to Eliott's apartment. Upon arrival, they are met by a large crowd standing in front of his building. They exit the car and walk quickly past the crowd. One person in the crowd shouts out something they never expected to hear.

"I can't wait until your concert. It will finally make others in the country music industry realize all music is for everyone, not just the straight country people. The LGBTQ need someone like you two to confirm what I have said."

Sam and Eliott stop in their tracks and look out into the crowd to see if they can find who said those words. They both felt they needed to reassure them that they would do exactly what they said, confirm that music is for everyone, not just straight people. But they could not tell who said it.

"We are not sure who just said that, but you are correct. We are doing this concert for everyone, not just gay people but straight people, too. Thank you for bringing what we want to accomplish to light," Eliott yells out to the crowd, hoping the person who said that would hear their response.

After Eliott speaks his thoughts to a true fan, they turn away and head to Eliott's apartment. Eliott opens the door for Sam to enter the apartment first. As Sam enters Eliott's apartment, he walks straight to the couch and crashes down on it. Sam is beginning to feel the aftermath of all the drinks the two of them drank and is having a hard time staying awake. Eliott notices how tired Sam is but he needs to speak to him before he passes out.

"Sam, are you planning on sleeping on the couch tonight or in my room?"

"If it's okay with you, may I sleep here? I don't think I can make it to your room right now."

"That's fine. I will get you some covers and a pillow. Give me a minute."

Eliott walks away, leaving Sam alone on the couch. He heads to his room to grab a good blanket and pillow for Sam. Eliott wants to be sure he is comfortable for the night because they have a big day tomorrow. They need to begin planning for their great performance coming up soon.

By the time Eliott returns to the living room, Sam is already naked and asleep on the couch. Eliott takes a moment to look over Sam's smooth-built, nude body before putting the covers over him. Eliott opens the covers and drapes them over Sam, slowly covering up Sam's exposed body. As he places the covers over Sam, he accidentally grazes Sam's member, causing Sam to reach down and grab Eliott's hand. Eliott quickly withdraws his hand from Sam's and spreads the covers over Sam. He then retreats to his room.

Eliott quickly undresses for bed. As soon as his head hits his pillow, he is out like a light.

The morning comes early for Eliott since he didn't close the curtains on his windows before going to bed. The sun shines brightly through the room. He slowly opens his eyes and suddenly smells breakfast in the air. Eliott wonders, 'How can Sam get up early enough to cook breakfast after the night we had?'

Eliott gets out of bed and without getting dressed, walks into the living room. He walks into the kitchen and is greeted by Sam, who is completely naked and cooking breakfast.

"Morning, Eliott. I hope you're hungry because I have cooked eggs, pancakes, biscuits, bacon, and even some country ham for breakfast."

"I didn't know I had all of that in my kitchen. Are you sure none of it has expired?" Eliott halfway says to Sam jokingly.

"I'm sure the food is all fine. Now, sit down, and I'll bring everything to you."

Eliott does as Sam instructed him to do and sits at the table. Sam brings breakfast to the table, sits, and they begin to eat. When they finally finish eating breakfast, Sam cleans up. Eliott goes to take a shower to get ready for a very busy day.

Sam finishes cleaning up after breakfast and enters the bathroom, not expecting to see Eliott still in the shower, but there he is. Sam decides to hop in the shower with Eliott.

"What are you doing?" Eliott questions Sam.

"Taking a shower. What brings you here?" Sam retorts to Eliott.

Eliott doesn't say anything to Sam because he knows Sam well enough to know when he is joking. Eliott continues to wash his hot, wet body with soap at the same time Sam brushes him as he passes beside him to get under the shower head. Once Sam is soaking wet, he moves past Eliott again to completely soap his body. With his body all soapy, Sam moves closer to Eliott and begins to help him finish washing off his freshly cleaned body. Eliott openly accepts Sam's help. Now that Eliott is all clean, he returns the favor to Sam, helping him wash soap all over his amazingly hot body until he is completely covered and ready to get rinsed off. Eliott grabs Sam by the waist and pulls him a little closer to his body until their naked bodies are pressed up against each other. Eliott suddenly begins to turn Sam towards the shower head, changing places with him in the shower, then releases him. When Sam has all the soap off his body, he reaches down to turn off the water so they can get out.

With the water turned off and steam filling the bathroom, Eliott walks over to the mirror and wipes it off with a hand towel. Sam and Eliott help dry each other off, and once they are both dry, they move to Eliott's bedroom so they can get dressed.

"Sam, we need to start preparing for the concert. We need to quickly prepare our song list and choose our outfits, as time is limited. For the next two weeks, we are not going out. We should stay either at my place or yours until we have everything figured out. How does that sound?" Eliott asks Sam.

"I have no problem being stuck in a room with you for two weeks. I am perfectly fine with your plan. I also want to be sure we do not make fools of ourselves in front of such a large crowd," Sam expresses to Eliott.

***

The day finally came for the performance Clara had set in motion for them. The crowd was growing at the venue, and more people were arriving for a sold-out concert for Sam and Eliott's first monumental performance. Sam and Eliott almost passed out when Clara told them their concert was a sell-out. They both felt ready to face their fans and also the haters. They were determined to challenge the idea that country music is only for straight people. They knew they were making history tonight. They had only another hour before taking the stage, so they kept practicing their new songs together.

Before they knew it, the time had come for them to take the stage and sing their hearts out to show everyone what it means to be loved and in love and not have to be straight to achieve such things. They were ready to make their actual debut on the country music scene.

Once Sam and Eliott took their places on the stage with curtains closed, they checked that the band Clara hired to play with them was ready. They began strumming their guitars for a song everyone already knew, 'Boots and Heartstrings,' their duet that started it all for them. As soon as they began to play, the crowd went wild, screaming and yelling for them to come out and play. Their fans were making it known they would always be fans of Sam and Eliott, which gave them the confidence they needed to make it through the night. It was all they needed.

Sam and Eliott continue playing their guitars as the curtains quickly open, exposing them to the loud, excited, joyful crowd that filled the venue. With the curtains open, they could see how many people were out there cheering for them. They shot a look of excitement at each other, knowing everything would be okay. Before Sam and Eliott began singing the words to 'Boots and Heartstrings,' the band quickly jumped in, amping up their music, moving it up into a league of its own. They were both surprised to see how much a band playing with them increased the quality of their songs and their energy to perform with such ferocity. That made the crowd go even more wild.

With the band backing them up, they continue playing their songs. The crowd was singing the songs they knew and screaming to the new songs they never heard. The entire venue was having an amazing time throughout the three-hour concert. After finishing their set, they thanked the crowd for coming out, making history with them, and having faith in their music. They made their exit off the stage. But the crowd was not ready for them to stop. They kept screaming, 'encore, encore, encore,' which left them with no choice but to go back out and perform another song for them. They felt they owed it to the crowd. They gave them what they wanted, another song. They walked back out on stage without the band so they could sing another new song they had written during their two-week separation from the outside world, 'Love Shines Bright.' It is a song about two people who the world felt should never be able to fall in love. But they did fall in love, and there was nothing the world could do to change how they felt about each other. It is the story of Sam and Eliott's love for each other.

Chapter 10

Encore

"I can't believe we met at my first open mic night at The Whiskey Factory. You may have noticed I was so nervous that night. I had no clue what I was doing. I was content with writing music for others. I was making a good living doing it. But for some reason, that night, I wanted to do something for myself. I still can't believe I sang that night," Eliott opens up to Sam.

"Can I tell you something?" Sam asks Eliott.

"Of course you can. What is it?" Eliott replies.

"No one at The Whiskey Factory knew you were nervous. We saw a confident, handsome young man on stage singing his heart out. It was the best night of my life. After watching you perform that night, I had to build up my courage to speak to you. It was the first time I ever felt insecure," Sam honestly tells Eliott.

"What! You have to be kidding. You are the most confident person I know. Why did my singing make you feel insecure? When you came over to me, I was in shock that you came over at all. I never had confidence in myself, hence writing songs for other stars. The songs those artists sang may have been my words, but they were the ones people were looking at, not me. I was content with that partnership."

"It's true. You were so open and honest with the words of your song that I couldn't help myself from being shy around you. You showed such confidence on stage, something I thought I had, but I realized that night I was nothing compared to you. You had the crowd eating out of your hand, hanging on to every word you sang. It was mesmerizing watching you on stage. You had my heart before we ever spoke to each other. Meeting you changed my life forever, not just in the music world but in my personal life, too. I knew then that I found the one I wanted to spend the rest of my life with. So, I mustered up the courage to walk over to talk to you, only to be confused as a waiter, if you can recall," Sam laughs at his last remark to Eliott.

"Don't remind me. I feel so bad about it now. I only thought you worked there because I never thought anyone would just come over to talk to me about music, much less anything else. You caught me off guard because I thought you were so beautiful, standing in front of me, looking like a waiter," Eliott plays with Sam's confidence again.

"Let's move past you thinking I was a waiter and on to our coffee meeting if you don't mind."

"If you insist. Why do you want to talk about our coffee meeting? Nothing out of the norm happened."

"For you, maybe, but for me, something did happen. For example, it was the night I got your number. Getting your number was a big moment in my life, getting the number of such an established songwriter in the country music industry. Not only that but the number of the hottest guy I had ever met."

"So, talking to me was just a ploy to get my number? A person who writes songs for famous singers. You are telling me this now, why?" Eliott is not pleased with what Sam has just told him.

"No, nothing like that. It was because we could text each other the next day before meeting again for your answer about collaborating with me. I had never needed to wait for someone to text me until I met you. I didn't care if they did. I have met many people over the years, but you are the only person I have ever waited to text me, but you never did. I had to text you first. I was never the first to text someone after meeting them until meeting you. You made me want to text you because I couldn't wait for you to text me, which was when I knew my life would never be the same again," Sam turns his head as he finishes the last sentence of his story.

Eliott is surprised to learn he somehow changed Sam, in a sense, from who he was before watching him sing.

"Sam, are you saying I changed you that night?"

"In a way, yes, but in the most amazing way. You gave me a reason to put someone else first. You were the first person I felt I needed to chase to get to know. Previously, I was always the one who got chased, but it never ended well. So, if I had to chase you, I would. My mind was made up, and I knew then you were the person who would make me into the best version of myself. I am grateful every day for the chance to pursue you, even if you never noticed I was pursuing you. I hope I am not freaking you out because I never stalked you. I never knew who you were until that night at The Whiskey Factory. It was love at first sight for me. I hope this is not creeping you out," Sam quickly tries to justify his actions.

"Sam, are you serious? That is such a crazy story, but can I tell you something? I fell in love with you when you walked up to my table after I sang for the first time when I thought you were a waiter. I have never felt such a powerful thing take over my heart and mind at the same time until I saw you standing in front of me. You sat and drank with me, which made me feel safe. That was the first time I ever felt safe with a man. That was the night I knew for sure I was gay because of how you made me feel at that moment. I never wanted it to end." Eliott tells Sam his true thoughts of the night they met and why he loves to think of Sam as his waiter that night.

"Are you upset with me?"

"How could I be upset when I was in love with you before you were with me? It's only because of our meeting and falling in love that we could go this far with our singing careers. Don't you agree?"

"I have to admit you are correct. Our lives changed in different ways, and I can see it now. You came out of the shadows to sing a song you wrote, and I changed because I learned I needed someone else to feel whole. You did that for me."

"So, the only question for us now is where do we go from here?" Eliott says to Sam.

"That's easy. We continue writing songs together and working on music that will resonate with our fans. We need to work on an album so we can reach more people. We are only reaching local fans. We need to go nationwide!" Sam replies to Eliott's question.

"Are you serious? Do you think we are ready for an album? We have only had one concert in a large venue. How do you know our music will be loved nationwide?" Eliott quickly begins to show his anxiety rising.

"Think about it, Eliott. If we have this many fans in Nashville, think of how many fans we could gain from all over the United States. We are in the country music capital of the world. We have overcome many obstacles. We should get our music out for people to hear in other parts of the country," Sam assures Eliott.

Eliott has to think about what Sam is telling him because he is unsure what to do. Then he replies to Sam.

"Let me call Clara and see what she thinks about this before we get in over our heads since we don't have a music producer yet. No matter what we do, we will pay for everything out of our pockets unless she can find us a label. Will you at least allow me to call her?"

"Of course. I know that without a label or someone to back our album, we will have to pay for everything and it's very expensive. I also want you to know I have saved some money to help with everything. I am not asking you to pay for everything. If we do this, we will go in as partners. I want you to know I have your back as long as you have mine," Sam reassures Eliott.

Eliott takes out his phone and calls Clara. They speak for over an hour, going back and forth about the costs, the time it will take them to record an album, and how hard it will be to find a record label willing to sign an openly gay country couple. Eliott explains to Clara the money is not an issue and if she can't acquire a label for them, they have no problem doing this on their own. They continue their conversation, but Sam can only hear one side. When Eliott hangs up, he walks over to Sam who is patiently sitting on the couch and sits next to him.

"Sam, I know you heard most of my conversation with Clara. Clara expects us to come up with several new songs to go along with the current songs that we sang during our concert. Once we have several songs we agree on, she wants us to schedule a time to sing all of our songs to her so she can pick what she thinks needs to go on the album. Before you say anything, understand she knows more about this industry than we do. If she wants a song on the album or a song to be left off the album, no matter how we feel about the song, what she says is final," Eliott tells Sam what Clara's terms are for helping them to create an album to release.

Sam leans back on the couch to let everything sink in before replying to Eliott. He has some reservations about giving Clara full authority over what will go on their album. He does not know Clara as well as Eliott and does not want to hurt his feelings, but he knows this is also about his career.

"Eliott, I want you to know that I am ready to create new songs and music with you, but I have doubts about Clara picking out what goes on our first album, regardless of how much experience she has in the industry. This album will be the first for both of us, and I don't know if I want to leave it up to Clara to decide what we release and what we don't, not on our first album. I will agree to Clara's terms with one addition. If we BOTH agree on something she doesn't, we will get to override her. I mean if we both have strong feelings about a song we write and sing to go on the album and she says "No," we get to say 'Yes.' If we don't get to have some say on our first album, then I will have to tell you I don't want her involved. I hope you understand where I am coming from here because it will not be only your first album, but mine as well. If I am going to fund half of it, I want some reassurance I have some say in it," Sam tells Eliott his honest thoughts on Clara.

At first, Eliott is taken aback by how Sam has reacted to receiving much-needed help from Clara. He stands up from the couch and walks away from Sam without saying anything to him. He needs a minute to put himself in Sam's shoes since Eliott has known Clara for several years and has always agreed with her opinion. The more he thinks about it, he can see how all of this may be new for Sam and walks back over to the couch.

"Sam, I understand. I know I may have been in the industry a little longer than you, behind the scenes, but I understand what you must be going through. I know you want to keep building on this high note from our concert, but you should think about how moving too fast can hurt a career. Not only mine, but yours. We should think about working on new music together and then go from there. We do not have to plan out our entire lives in one night. After such an amazing concert, we are both running on endorphins and alcohol, so making a life decision should not be something we should do right now. We need some time to be ourselves while continuing to create new music. I don't want us to forget who we are as individuals and as a couple. Are you okay with us slowing down a little to focus on us and new music, and not the future of our singing careers?" Eliott openly asks Sam.

Suddenly, Sam realized he was moving way too fast and agreed with Eliott to move a little slower. He became embarrassed about his actions over the last two hours. He needed to apologize to Eliott.

"Eliott, I am so sorry about all of this. You are right, I need to slow down and not make life decisions for the both of us after a concert. Thank you for reminding me that I am new to all of this, and I should respect your input based on your experience in the industry. With that said, when we do get to the point of releasing an album, I want us to have some say about what songs go on the album. I want our first album to be something we came up with and agreed on, not someone else making all the decisions. I hope you can understand why I want this." Sam apologizes to Eliott while agreeing with his opinion.

Eliott smiles at Sam and reaches over to give him a big hug. Sam hugs him back, tightly, and softly rubs Eliott's back.

Sam whispers in Eliott's ear, "I don't know what I would do without you," then softly kisses his neck.

Eliott feels shivers running down his back as Sam makes his way from kissing his neck to slowly making his way up to his ear. Once Sam's mouth is next to Eliott's ear, Sam begins to softly blow into his ear, which causes Eliott to feel things he never felt before. The next moment Eliott grabs Sam by the back of his neck, forcing him to do the next logical thing he can think of. Sam sticks his tongue into Eliott's ear and slowly moves it around his ear lobes. The motion of Sam's tongue inside Eliott's ears causes him to push Sam back onto the sofa to the point Eliott is lying on top of him, kissing him all over his neck as well. This goes on until both of their mouths reach each other's mouth and they begin to kiss in a very intense way. This is a first for Eliott and he was enjoying every minute of it.

The night goes on until early morning, and eventually, they both fall asleep. After such a wonderful night together, they sleep for most of the day. Eliott wakes up before Sam and decides that, since Sam usually cooks breakfast for them, he will take the initiative this time. Eliott gets up and heads to the kitchen.

Eliott did not bother putting anything on as he was making breakfast, even though it was 4:00 in the evening. He was cooking away feverishly for half an hour before he was surprised by Sam waking in the kitchen, undressed as well.

"Sam, what are you doing awake and walking into the kitchen? I was trying to make breakfast in bed for you," Eliott quickly says to Sam.

"Bed? We slept on the couch," Sam replies to Eliott with a huge smile.

"Fine, breakfast on the couch. Is that better?"

"It doesn't sound better, but it is the truth. So, do you want me to return to the couch and wait for breakfast, or should I sit at the table?"

"You better get your ass back to the couch, and when I am finished cooking, I will bring it to you," Eliott instructs Sam, and he obeys.

Eliott takes Sam his breakfast on the couch, and the two sit close together. As they ate, they let their conversation last night about an album simmer until they could devise a plan.

Chapter 11

Reprise

It has been two months since their tremendous performance in Nashville, and Eliott and Sam have been living on cloud nine. They have had to endure criticism from their haters and religious groups. While they have their share of haters, they know it comes with the territory of being a star. They are happy they converted several former haters into fans after their performance. Articles in the local paper and interviews on television confirmed several of their previous adversaries were now allies to their cause. They recognized the music Sam and Eliott were singing was not only for the LGBTQ community but for anyone who has or has had feelings for someone else.

Even though they survived their concert, they knew they had to deliver more music while maintaining their public relationship. Eliott has only heard from Clara a few times about them putting an album together. Things are going great between Eliott and Sam, and neither could imagine singing or writing songs without the other one.

Their love continues to grow, and their fans can see it. They took a short break after their concert to have time for each other and to create new music for a hopeful upcoming album. They didn't want to let their fame come between their love for each other. During their hiatus from the spotlight, they strengthened their relationship and worked on their music equally.

Eliott and Sam still had their separate apartments, but they were spending more time staying at Eliott's place. They did go out a couple of times a week but refrained from singing at open mic nights. They wanted to keep out of the spotlight for the time being, enabling them the time to work on music together. Eliott's songwriting for other stars has begun to pick up since their concert, allowing Sam to cut his hours to part-time at the record label where he works. Sam going part-time was his choice, not Eliott's. Sam was able to go part-time because he had enough money saved up over the years that allowed him to continue supporting himself.

Sam decided to go part-time at work mainly so he would have time to work on songs for him and Eliott to sing. He did not create complete songs but came up with ideas and some lyrics he could present to Eliott to see if it was something he could write about. Their relationship transformed into a partnership, not just a relationship, which was what they both wanted. They each are committed to making their life together the best life either of them ever had. They want to become the next country music power couple. Just loving each other or just working together would not make that possible. They need a loving and working partnership to let the country industry know how serious they are about each other and their music.

Eliott's new clients were already country music superstars who learned about Eliott after hearing about his and Sam's concert. A couple of Eliott's clients attended that concert and found themselves loving every single minute of it. They loved the songs the pair sang and were jealous because Eliott didn't write those songs for them. That led those clients to spread the word throughout the country music scene about how well-written their songs were. While many singers may have the same music manager, they may never know who their manager's other clients are. When they expressed to their managers how much they loved Eliott and Sam's songs, those managers told their other clients about the new duo on the country music scene. Those clients began looking for anyone who may have filmed the concert so they could see what all the fuss was about. With footage found, they watched what they could. Then, all of them wanted Eliott to write songs for them. That all led to their managers reaching out to Clara. The country music industry is a tight-knit community. Eliott's client list began to grow so fast that he had to limit the number of songs he would help write for each new client.

Eliott loves writing songs for other people. Even though he was in the process of repositioning himself in Nashville, Eliott wanted to keep writing for others. Many of the songs Eliott wrote were for specific artists rather than songs he would write for himself or Sam. Hearing the songs sung by those clients gives him a sense of appreciation. Eliott wants a backup plan if he and Sam do not make it big.

When Sam had to work, Eliott would schedule his secession with his clients on those same days. Eliott has taken charge of his work life. He was clear with his clients that when he said their session was over for the day, he meant it. At night, after both of their workdays, Sam and Eliott didn't spend it talking about music or even working on their music. Those evenings were for them to be present with each other. On those evenings, they have begun going out again to eat, watch a movie, or even back to open mic nights to sing together or solo. They wanted to make the best effort to support each other as individuals, not just as a couple. There have been several times on their nights out together that their fans continually let them know just how much of a fan they are to them. On other nights, their critics expressed their feelings towards them. It was hard at first for them to go out and listen to all the comments coming from both sides, but they learned how to deal with it. They never said anything negative to their haters and only positive things to their fans.

On the nights they sang at open mic night, they made sure to sing songs they had been working on that neither wanted on their new album. They were not bad songs, but they had already come up with so many better songs. The ones they sang might make it on their next album if they were lucky enough to have a second album. It did not matter what the two of them sang those nights because everyone in the bar they were at loved every song. They constantly had drinks brought to their table if they sang together or brought over to their table when the other sang alone. They always assured their fans that they were collaborating on some other new things for them, and in due time, they would release the big news about their project. Those announcements always made their fans go wild.

One night, when they went out, they were met by an angry crowd who despised their music and disagreed with their lifestyle. On that particular evening, they were leaving Sam's flat. As soon as they walked out of the building, the crowd was already there with signs that read, 'Gays are against God', 'Gays go to HELL', 'Watch your children', and even 'GOD hates GAYS'. Even though they both knew how to handle those groups by ignoring them, it still didn't stop one of the crowd members from throwing pig's blood all over Eliott. With the pig's blood all over his head and shirt, he kept his head high and just walked past them, showing no sign of emotion. Eliott decided to go about his business the rest of the day with the blood still all over him. He wanted others to see just how poorly gay people were treated in the United States. Eliott wanted to let those same people know that no matter what they did to him, it would not stop him from going shopping, to the post office, or anywhere else he wanted to go. He would live his life to the fullest, regardless of how others felt about his lifestyle. Eliott often wondered why those groups focused so much on a gay person's life. He knew being a gay man, he never worried about straight people's lives, except to hope they were happy in their lives. Neither Sam, Eliott, nor any other person in the LGBTQ community understood why other people were so upset about their community. Everyone who identified as part of the community wondered why. Why were straight religious groups so focused on a person who is gay? What did they have to gain from being so angry? Why were laws created to discriminate against the community? Why do they care? It is still unclear to everyone in the LGBTQ community why others were so angry about something that has nothing to do with them or their religions.

Eliott and Sam's fans could see just how brave they were by Eliott not going back upstairs to change that day but continuing with his plans for the day. That inspired not only the LGBTQ community in Nashville but also many of their straight fans. Many of their supporters began to go out with red paint all over their heads and shirts, showing support for Sam and Eliott, and no matter what any anti-gay group did to anyone in the LGBTQ community, it would never force them back into a closet.

Seeing their fans imitate Eliott's actions inspired them to write new songs. Eliott and Sam wanted to show their fans appreciation and respect. Neither of them ever expected regular people in Nashville to become so involved in protecting the LGBTQ community. They created several songs for all of their supporters. There were so many songs that they knew they would never be able to get them all on their first album, so they began singing many of those songs on open mic nights.

Once people understood the lyrics of their new songs, more and more people began coming to their open mic nights. So many people attended the bars where they were singing that they had to stop letting people in, which created large groups outside each bar. Their popularity grew so much that the bars began setting up large TVs outside their bars so everyone could watch them perform. That, in turn, started a war between the bars to see who could create the best outside area for guests to watch, not only them but all performers at their bars. With everything going on between the bars to be the best, Sam and Eliott were the most sought-after duo to perform at any bar in Nashville. With their popularity rising again, people also requested them to perform at their gay weddings, bar openings, and even birthday parties. It all started well but became a burden to them both.

Being pursued by influential individuals in Nashville caused them to distance themselves from their special intimate evenings meant only for the two of them. They were no longer singing solo and supporting each other, only singing together as requested. This shift in their relationship caused them to realize they were moving away from what they wanted for themselves, so they slowly began to turn down paying gigs at the bars to get back to focusing on each other. They both knew they had their entire lives ahead of them. Now was not the time to drift apart; it was a time for them to bond more. So that is what they did. They stopped going out and focused on each other and their music.

Chapter 12

Duet in Life

Once Eliott and Sam decided to get back to focusing on themselves, they realized they wasted so much time by going from Sam's place to Eliott's place every so often. They both knew how they wanted to move their relationship to the next level, but neither of them wanted to be the first to suggest it. They beat around the bush with each other hoping the other would suggest them moving in together, but neither of them ever did. While they both became frustrated with each other, they never let the other know why they were frustrated. It was a total miscommunication between them. Until Eliott decided he was going to suggest.

"Sam, can we sit down and talk for a minute? I must ask a serious question."

"Of course, love. What's on your mind?"

"Well, you know, we each have separate apartments, and while we spend more time at my place, I think we should move in together. How do you feel about us moving in together?"

"Are you serious?"

"Yes. Do you not feel the same way?"

"Of course I do. I have been hinting for several months that we should move in together. Have you not noticed my hints?"

"Have you not noticed mine? I have been hinting around to you that we should, but you never seemed to react to what I was saying. So, you do agree we should move in together. Is that what I am hearing?"

"Absolutely!" Sam exclaims to Eliott.

"Thank God you agree. I feared you would not want to move in here with me." Eliott thinks he understood what Sam had said.

"What? I thought you would move in with me at my place. Do you not want to move in with me?" Sam corrects Eliott.

They both quickly begin to laugh at each other, because to be honest, it didn't matter to either of them whose place they lived in as long as they were living together. When they stopped laughing, Eliott tried to convince Sam to move into his place.

"Sam, as you know, I own my place, but you are paying rent where you live. I think the best option is for you to end your lease and move in here with me. After you move in, it will become our place, because I will add you to the mortgage deed. That way we are owners, together, and not you just living with me. We will be truly living together."

Eliott suggests to Sam the benefits of moving to his place instead of Sam's.

"Well, if you think about it that way, if we sold your place and you moved in with me, we will have the money from selling your place for our upcoming album if we decide to proceed. I'm not saying I want your money, because you know I have my own money for the album. I think it would be a great nest egg for us if we buy an actual house instead of a condo," Sam counters Eliott's suggestion.

They continue to discuss the benefits of the other giving up their place to move into the other place for the rest of the day. They were both getting aggravated with the other, but not in an actual upsetting way. Instead, it was more of a battle of who has the best reasons. They began to play games together and the one who won would be the one whose place where they would move. They started with 'rock, paper, scissors,' then progressed to poker. That led to shooting pool at a local pool hall. The more they played, the more they tied. Neither wanted to give up their place at first. Then Sam finally agreed to end his lease and move into Eliott's place. He had always known he would move in with Eliott. He would go anywhere to be with him. Sam was merely playing the games because it was the most fun, they had had since all their fame began.

"Eliott, I am happy to end my lease and move in with you. I didn't want the fun to end, so I kept challenging you to another game and another. If you have not noticed, it has kept our minds off the album, the fans, the critics, and anything else we were worried about. We were having a great time and enjoying each other's company just as we used to, before all of this. I hope you are not upset with me," Sam jokingly tells Eliott.

Eliott said nothing to Sam, he just smiled at him with pure happiness. He had felt Sam was playing a game and honestly didn't want it to end either. Eliott loved playing any game Sam suggested, especially when he suggested strip poker. That night got a little wild, so they never knew who finally won, but they both felt it was a tie and knew it didn't matter.

"So, we have decided. You will end your lease and gain a mortgage with me. I love you so much and thank you for the games. The games made this so much better because it means I won strip poker," Eliott quickly tells Sam with a huge smile.

"That game is still a tie. We will have to play at least one more to determine the winner. That will be the first game we play on game night after I move in officially," Sam tells Eliott, who was not bothered by the demand.

"Fine, we will have a tiebreaker the night you move in for good," Eliott agrees with Sam.

It would take two months before Sam was fully moved into Eliott's place because he had to give a sixty-day notice to end his lease. During those two months, they slowly moved more, and more of Sam's things into Eliott's place. Eliott has a large two-bedroom two-bath condo overlooking downtown Nashville. It was in a better location than Sam's place, making it an easy move for Sam.

Finally, the day had come when they were officially living together. Eliott placed a deck of cards on the dining room table, hoping to surprise Sam with their first game night since living together.

Sam walks into the dining room and notices Eliott sitting at the table with an unusual number of clothes on and a deck of cards sitting on the table.

"Eliott? Am I missing something here?" Sam asks.

"What? Did you forget already? Remember that we said when you were officially moved in, we would have a tiebreaker for our strip poker game. Or would you prefer we just kept unpacking your boxes tonight?" Eliott suggestively responds to Sam.

Sam looks at the deck of cards and then at Eliott sitting at the table. He looks over at his unpacked boxes and chooses the game with Eliott.

Sam quickly sits at the table, not going to his room to put on more clothes. He was only wearing jogging pants and a tank top tee shirt. He was barefooted and was wearing nothing underneath his joggers.

"You are right. It's time for our tiebreaker. Do you want to deal, or should I?"

"You deal because you know I don't know how," Eliott resentfully tells Sam.

Sam quickly takes the deck of cards into his hands and shuffles them. Once they were shuffled, he dealt out each of their hands. Then he told Eliott, "We are playing Texas Hold'em. We both get two cards. Then, we bet on the cards we have in our hands. Then we bet on the cards we have in our hands; plus, the cards I flip over during the game. I will burn the first card, then place a card face down on the table. You will see how your cards match the face-up card on the table, then bet. Then, I will burn another card before revealing another face-up card on the table. You do the same thing you did in the first round. I will continue this process until five cards are face up on the table. You will then make the best hand out of the two cards you have with the five face-up cards on the table. If you have the worst hand, you must remove an article of clothing. Do you understand the rules of the game?" Sam informs Eliott of the rules of the game before they begin.

"Oh, I understand completely. Now, deal the cards," Eliott demands of Sam.

Sam begins to deal out the cards for their first game. With the cards dealt, they bet, both thinking they will beat the other. To no one's surprise, Sam wins the first hand, so Eliott has to remove an article of clothing. Eliott does as the game rules instruct and removes his shoes. They continue the game, with Sam winning almost every hand. By this point in the game of strip poker, Sam is down to just his jogging pants, with Eliott down to his underwear. It becomes obvious to Eliott that Sam knows more about Texas Hold'em than he does, but he doesn't mind. Now that they are both down to their last article of clothing, Sam deals the final hand, winner takes all, and he meant it. When the last card is dealt face up on the table, Eliott bets all, forcing Sam to do the same. It was the only way for the game to end. Both of them have already built up enough sexual pressure to win. Neither cared who won. They just wanted the game to end. To Sam's surprise, Eliott has the winning hand, forcing Sam to remove his last article of clothing, his jogging pants.

Sam removes his joggers, and before he can congratulate Eliott for winning, Eliott is all over

Sam like a cheap suit. Eliott had already removed his underwear, and the both of them were standing naked in the dining room. One thing led to another as they headed to their bedroom. With their hot, sweaty bodies caressing each other, they could not resist the appeal they had for each other. They made love before falling asleep next to each other in the home they would build together from that moment on.

In the beginning, things between them went smoothly, until they didn't. After a month, their work schedules began to clash. Eliott's clients became more insistent on his working with them more often and for longer sessions. Sam stayed longer at the office doing more and more work for the record label. It began to stress each of them out, causing them to argue. They were never real arguments, but it was enough to irritate them both. Over time, they both knew they had to find a resolution.

"Eliott, I know your clients are important to you, but you must set boundaries with them. They are here every day and stay for hours on end. We have no time for each other anymore," Sam conveyed to Eliott.

"So, is this all my fault? Look at you, staying at work all day, almost every day now, even though you are part-time," Eliott tells Sam.

"I only stay at work now because I'm worried one of your clients may be here when I get home. I have to admit, at first, I was thrilled to see your clients at the house. Your clients are artists I have admired for so many years, but after a while, it gets old. Don't they understand you are also trying to live your life, your life with me?" Sam elaborates to Eliott.

It became obvious between them that they each had issues with the other. They knew then they needed to get back to focusing on themselves. They had let their work take over their lives again, taking them off course on their personal goals. One of their goals was to put out an album of their music and have a life together. They agreed to reduce their workloads and get back to working on the music for their album.

Clara had already informed Eliott she had found a label to sign them, but they only had two months to get their songs together. That was almost two months ago. They both felt the pressure of finishing the songs that they and Clara could agree upon for the album. So far, it has been tough to get Clara to concur on the songs they wanted. She wanted more upbeat songs, while they both wanted more heartfelt songs. They finally agreed to put at least seven upbeat and five heartfelt songs on the album. It felt like a win for Clara as well as a win for Sam and Eliott.

After the discussion they had with each other about how their work lives were talking over, and they both agreed to reduce their workloads, they were quickly back on track to complete the songs for their album. When they finally finished the last song for Clara to vote on for the album, they felt confident in their final works of art. Clara, on the other hand, was not so pleased with their last song and demanded they go back to the drawing board for a final song. That was only two days from their deadline with the label who wanted to sign them. They both knew they needed to impress the label. So, they went back and looked over several of the songs they had already written. They decided to combine a few of those songs into one fabulous, upbeat song Clara could not veto. They worked all night on their last-minute artistic creation, hoping it would be enough to win Clara's approval.

The next morning, they were prepared to perform the song mashup they had created the night before. Clara agreed to hear their last-ditch effort to produce a song she would allow on their album. Clara came over to their place so they could play for her and let her hear what they had come up with. By the time they ended the song, Clara was starstruck. She could not believe her ears of what she had just heard. She told them it was their best work ever, and they were then ready to pitch their songs to the label.

Clara took them to a recording studio to record their new song to add to their album so she would have a finished product to present to the label. After listening to them perform their latest song, Clara jumped up and down in excitement. Clara could not believe what she had just listened to. She knew they had an album any record label would want to produce. Clara was so confident in their album that she decided to push back the meeting with the label that had already agreed to produce their album. If they liked it, they would send it to every record label, not only in Nashville but in California as well. She was not about to make Sam and Eliott settle for one offer on their music. She wanted a bidding war between labels.

Sam and Eliott were not happy with Clara's decision to postpone the meeting with the label that had already agreed to produce their album to expand their label pool. They had no idea what Clara was thinking, but they soon learned it was a great ploy. Before they knew it, they began receiving offers from many record labels who all wanted to produce their album. Then, the bidding wars began. They were so surprised to see how much the record labels were offering to pay to be the record label to be the first to produce their music. Neither of them had ever seen offers with so many zeros in them. It was up to them to decide who they wanted to go with. They then knew they had a little time until a decision had to be made, but they didn't waste any time before choosing one.

Chapter 13

Stardust Serenades

Eliott and Sam took a couple of weeks to decide which record label they wanted to sign with. They had researched all the bidding record labels before making a final decision. They wanted to be sure the label they signed with would not take advantage of them for their benefit. Once they decided, Eliott called Clara to inform her which record label they wanted to represent them.

"Clara, we have decided on the label we want to use to produce our album. We have chosen Eagle Records. Do you mind calling them to inform them we have chosen them?" Eliott asks Clara.

"Are you both sure you want Eagle Records as your label?" Clara responds to Eliott.

"We are, but why are you asking?"

"I am only asking because they did not have the highest offer."

"We didn't choose them based on their offer. We chose them because they had the best reviews from artists, and I have also asked all of my clients who they were with. A few of my clients do not seem happy with their labels, and several of those labels were the highest offers. We chose them because, from the reviews and the clients I have who are on the same label, they make their clients happier than the ones with the highest offer."

"Wow! You two must be the first artists not all about the money. I must say, this surprises me," Clara admits to Eliott.

"You are correct. It is not all about the money. It's about our happiness," Eliott relays to Clara.

Clara accepts their choice and ends the call with Eliott. As soon as she hung up with Eliott, she contacted Derek Hall, the owner of Eagle Records.

***

Derek is the conservative veteran county music singer who started the rumor on national television that Eliott and Sam's music was stolen from Eliott's clients. Of course, Sam and Eliott have no clue that Derek owns Eagle Records, but Derek is all too aware of who Sam and Eliott are.

"Hello, Clara. I hope you have some good news for me," Derek says as he answers his phone.

"I do. But I still don't know why you want to sign Sam and Eliott. You used to support them until they came out as a couple. What do you hope to accomplish by signing them now?" Clara questions Derek.

"May I be honest with you, Clara? I have no ill will towards Sam or Eliott. Yes. I may have had an issue with their relationship when it first came out, but their music is the real deal. I will never let my personal beliefs get in the way of signing the best artists. I have no other agenda for the couple except to make their dreams come true. You didn't tell them I was the one who put in the bid, did you?" Derek explains to Clara with a question.

"No, I didn't tell them about you. I have always let my clients make their own decisions regarding their futures. But if I find out you are out to hurt them, I will let them know," Clara threatens Derek.

"I promise you this, Clara, I would never hurt my clients. I am here to make money, and they are a gold mine. Trust me. You will soon find out," Derek reassures Clara his intentions are pure for Sam and Eliott.

Clara tells Derek to draw up the contract and send it to her office so she can have Eliott and Sam sign it. Then she hangs up with Derek.

***

"Sam, I can't believe we are signing with a real label. And we will soon have an album released."

"I know. I still can't wrap my head around it. I am still processing it all."

The two of them ran to each other and embraced. They share a passionate kiss, expressing their love for each other. There is so much to do now, but at this moment, there are no worries.

Within the next few weeks, they signed their contract with Eagle Records. Afterward, they were directed to come into the studio to begin recording their songs for their album. The excitement of being signed has worn off, and they are now in business mode. They knew they had to perform like never before.

Even though Sam worked for a record label in the past, this was his first time inside an actual recording studio. Just walking into the room caused Sam to get nervous. He was afraid he would not be able to perform under such pressure, but Sam knew he could not let Eliott down. This was the beginning of a new life together as partners and lovers.

Eliott, on the other hand, had been in several recording studios. He often attended recording sessions with his clients in case any unforeseen changes came up with the songs he had written for them. Even with Eliott's experience watching one of his clients in the sound booth recording his songs, he had never been in one. That caused his anxiety to rise. He took a moment to regain control over his emotions because he did not want to disappoint Sam. Neither knew the other was having issues with letting the other one down. That is how strong their connection and their love were for each other.

Sam and Eliott still did not know Derek Hall was the Eagle Records owner because they only dealt with Clara and the recording producers in the studio. Early in their recording sessions, it was clear to the producer that they were extremely nervous. Since the producer has worked with so many artists in the past, he was sure he could find a way to ease their nerves. One day before their session, he sat them down and reassured them they had nothing to fear. He informed them that he had seen this in many other artists he had recorded, and it all worked out for them. He gave them a little advice to overcome their fears of being recorded and assured them he would never steer them in the wrong direction. He was there to help them. His advice was what they needed to hear because, from that day on, their recording sessions went on without a hint of nerves.

It only took Sam and Eliott a couple of months to finish recording their debut album, but they knew the producer still had to do his job and make the album perfect. They had nothing left to do but wait.

While they waited for a finished album, they planned a private concert for their friends and family. They needed to do something to show them how much they appreciated each and every one of them. They wanted to show them how their support, through the years, had guided them to where they were now in life. They had the perfect venue in mind, The Whiskey Factory, the bar where they first met.

Sam took it upon himself to make the arrangements at The Whiskey Factory since he knew the owner. The owner of The Whiskey Factory had never had any artist offer to rent out the entire bar before and was eager to fulfill Sam's request, but she had one stipulation. The owner requested that their performance that night be on the TVs in her newly designed outside area. She assured Sam none of the outside guests would be able to get into the bar itself, but it was an opportunity for her to show her appreciation to them by allowing their fans a place to enjoy such an intimate event. She promised Sam, she would only stream them performing their songs, not the moments they spend with their friends and family. She agreed to stream only the songs they wanted others to hear, knowing they had an album coming out soon.

Sam agreed to her terms. His payment also included the outside bar drinks their fans would drink that night. After all, their fans also needed to be thanked for sticking by them during the harsh time with Derek Hall's comments on TV and the incident outside of Sam's flat when an angry mob was outside of his building and poured pig's blood all over Eliott. The way their fans came together and began wearing red paint over their heads and shirts to show their support for Sam and Eliott did not go unnoticed by them.

With the plans made for their private concert at The Whiskey Factory, the only thing left was back to waiting. While they waited, they met with the music producer to listen to each song as it was finished. They were there to see if there was anything they wanted to change or to approve the work already done. During those meetings, they were very impressed with the finished products. That's when they knew they made the best decision for their record label.

After a few weeks, the final album was ready to be released. They had high hopes for their album, but still feared many people were not accepting their music because of their love for each other. They also knew every artist faced the same fears. There would also be people who liked something and people who didn't like it for one reason or another. That knowledge helped them deal with their emotions because they would be subjected to the same fears other big artists have faced. That made them feel they had already succeeded in the country music industry.

Time passes, and they begin seeing advertisements about the debut album with pre-sales already open. The sight of those ads excited them even more. They still could not believe their album was already being sold in record numbers. They were informed by their representative with Eagle Records that their album was now the highest-selling pre-order sales the label had ever had with any of their clients. They were an overnight success, and the sales of their album reaffirmed it. They had made it into the country music world. They were the first openly gay couple with a top-selling debut album in country music history. They were beside themselves with all the attention they began to see.

Sam and Eliott were showcased on several nationwide late-night talk shows. So many people wanted to know everything about them; how they met, what drew them to each other, and how hard their journey had been. They openly told the hosts of each show their truth. They fell in love the first time they saw each other, and how Eliott mistook Sam for a waiter after he sang his first time on stage at The Whiskey Factory. They also let the hosts know just what they had to go through because of people like Derek Hall and the hate group who threw pig's blood on Eliott as he was leaving their home. They wanted to put a positive spin on each of those events by letting everyone know that no matter how hard life gets for you to achieve your dream, it is still possible. All you have to do is keep doing what you love and never let anyone tell you who or what you can and can't do. Eliott and Sam are proof of that.

Their message was getting out to not only the LGBTQ community but also to those who just didn't have faith in themselves. The two of them began to see support from other agencies, like those who helped bullied children, domestic violence victims' groups, and much more. This let them know that their suffering and obstacles were all worth it. They faced hate and love and survived.

After their tour of late-night talk shows ended, their album was released to the public. Their songs played on almost every country music radio station all over the United States. After the album release, they continued to show love and support towards each other in public, letting the world know they were never going to hide who they were, never again.

The day finally came for the private concert with their friends and family at The Whiskey Factory. Sam had decided to allow the owner to stream every song they sang that night because their album was already out. Why not let their fans experience such a personal event with them?

Sam and Eliott warmly invited all those who stood by them and offered unwavering support throughout their journey: their parents, cousins, aunts, uncles, and even several of their previous schoolteachers. They secretly owe much of their lives to those teachers. They were the first ones who saw their potential, not because of being gay or straight, but because of their talent. Their friend's list was not as grand as their family lists, but they both had very close friends they wanted to share the night with, so they were all invited.

Someone from Eagle Records supplied limousines to pick up every guest from the airports, hotels, or the homes of the local friends they invited. Neither Sam nor Eliott knew who sent the limos, but they were grateful for the offer. There was even a limo waiting for them when they exited their home.

As they walked up to the limo waiting for them, the driver stepped out of the front seat and went to the back of the car to open the door. As soon as they were in the back, they noticed someone sitting with them. They quickly realized it was Derek Hall, a person who tried to ruin their music careers.

"What are you doing here, Derek?" Eliott expressed anger in his tone.

"Relax, Eliott, it's not what you think," Derek quickly ushers for him to calm down. Once Eliott was leaning back into his seat, Derek spoke again. "I know you both have a reason to be upset with me, but please allow me to express my most sincere apologies to each of you. I know I came off harsh at first, but I can also tell you that your music has changed a few things within me. You both may have difficulty believing me, but it's true."

"What kind of changes, exactly, Derek?" Sam inquires of Derek.

"Look, I need you both to know that I own Eagle Records. I submitted the bid for your consideration because I recognize talent in both of you. I only want the best for you both, and with that, it helps me as well. I have heard your music, and I do enjoy every song. Your lifestyle may be against my own beliefs, but your talent together is nothing to be overlooked. That is why I bid to record your album. I know you have done your research and background check on Eagle Records, and the truth is my clients are happy. I will never do anything to disrupt any of my client's success. I will do what I can to help their success. Your success reflects on me as well. If you are doing good, then my business is doing good. But if you are beginning to fail, then my business suffers. I will never let my business suffer, so you will always have my full support in your career. I hope, if you can't accept my apology, you would at least believe I am here for you," Derek explained to them both.

Sam nor Eliott could believe what they were hearing from Derek. They began to wonder how they never knew Derek was the owner of Eagle Records. After a short discussion between the three on their way to The Whiskey Factory, they all agreed they needed a longer conversation about everything later. Tonight was their night with friends and family, and Derek was not invited.

When the limo stopped at The Whiskey Factory, the three agreed to continue their conversation later. Eliott and Sam would entertain friends and family for the night, and they exited the limo. The two of them resolved that they would not let the knowledge of Derek being their supporter now take away from what they had planned for the night. They were there to celebrate with their friends and family, something they felt they needed to do.

To their surprise, once again, when they exited the back of the limo, there was a large group of their fans outside of The Whiskey Factory. There were so many fans that they could not see all of them. Their supporters filled the streets and walkways of The Whiskey Factory, inundating them with happiness. They waved at their fans, signed a few autographs, and happily walked into the bar. As they entered The Whiskey Factory, they quickly noticed everyone they had invited to their private concert had shown up.

That was the moment when they realized they would make their lifelong dreams come true.

About the Author

Robert Starnes was born in a small town in Northeast Texas, where his journey with the written word began. In middle school, he discovered a love for writing short stories, a passion that blossomed despite the challenges he faced with dyslexia. To overcome his learning disability, Robert immersed himself in reading books that were adapted into movies, exploring the differences between the written and visual narratives. This practice not only improved his understanding of language but also enriched his appreciation for storytelling.

With a professional background in customer service and property management that spans over 24 years, Robert's experiences bring depth and authenticity to his writing. His diverse career has given him a keen insight into human nature, which is reflected in his characters and storylines.

Robert's first published work was *The Multifamily Housing Guide – Leasing 101* in 2016, a guide aimed at assisting new leasing professionals in the multifamily housing industry. His guide provided practical tools and advice to help them succeed in their new career, making their transition easier and more efficient.

Building on his early success, Robert ventured into the world of fiction, writing the *Saving*

History Series, a young adult historical fiction series. The five-book series has earned him the title of #1 best seller on Amazon, and the second book of the series debuted at #64 on Barnes & Noble's top 100. His novels draw inspiration from the past, present, and future, offering readers captivating and thought-provoking narratives.

'Echoes in Whispering Pines' was Robert's attempt at a murder mystery in a small town, proving his ever-expanding genres of Novellas and Novels.

Robert broke out into Science Fiction when he wrote A.N.D.R.E. (Advanced Neural-Based Digital Reasoning Entity) (Sept. 2024), a novel about the rise and fall of Artificial Intelligence in the future. While humans were forced to move underground the surface of the Earth to live, A.I.B.s (Artificial Intelligence Being) reigned over the surface for decades, until one of the first A.I.B.s, Andre made his way to a human colony with a plan to end the A.I.B.s rule over the surface.

John Grisham is one of Robert's favorite authors, though he also finds inspiration in the works of Suzanne Collins, Stephenie Meyer, Dan Brown, and Jobie Hughes. In his spare time, Robert enjoys baking cakes, reading, and working in property management.

Robert Starnes continues to captivate readers with his storytelling, blending his unique perspective and experiences into each work. Be sure to watch for his upcoming books and projects!

Books by Robert Starnes

'Echoes in Whispering Pines' – Starnes Books LLC (2024)
'A.N.D.R.E.' – Starnes Books LLC (2024)

Saving History Series

'Time Keeper' – Starnes Books LLC (2018)
'School Bound' – Starnes Books LLC (2019)
'Search Begins' – Starnes Books LLC (2019)
'Loose Ends' – Starnes Books LLC (2019)
'Final Hour' – Starnes Books LLC (2021)

The Multifamily Housing Guide Series

'Leasing 101: Garden Style' – Starnes Books LLC (2018)
'Assistant Manager 101' – Starnes Books LLC (2023)

Books Published by Starnes Books LLC

'Novel Study – Time Keeper' – Patricia Carpenter (2018)
'Trip of a Lifetime' – Eric K. Reinholt (2020)
'Moving On From Life's Challenges' – Mindy Briggs (2022)

Editing completed by

Carpenter Editing Services, Inc.